The Secrets of Seduction

The Ladies of the Burling School

Elizabeth Lennox

ISBN13: 9798657188103

This is a work of fiction. Names, characters, businesses, places, events, and incidents are either the product of the author's imagination or used in a fictitious manner. Any resemblance to actual persons, living or dead, or actual events is purely coincidental. Any duplication of this material, either electronic or any other format, either currently in use or a future invention, is strictly prohibited, unless you have the direct consent of the author.

Table of Contents

Chapter 1

The elegance and respectful hum of conversation in the upscale restaurant shattered without warning. Malcolm turned his head, startled. But as soon as he took in the three lovey ladies hugging and chatting excitedly, his irritation disappeared. Ella!

"Do you know those ladies, my lord?" his companion asked indignantly, obviously just as affronted by the interruption as Malcolm.

As soon as the beautiful ladies pulled away, his eyes focused on one in particular. Ella Fleming. She was back and...shockingly, more beautiful than ever. If Malcolm hadn't seen her himself, he wouldn't have believed it was possible.

"Who are they?" the older man demanded, looking disgruntled as he twisted in his chair to get a better look at the noisy group. "Is that...?" the man asked, his outrage dissipating as his mouth hung open in shock.

"Yes. That is Queen Cassandra del Soya Irazi and Naya Danilov."

"Oh," he took a longer look at the trio. "I've wanted to speak with Pierce Danilov for ages!" Shaking his nearly bald head, he sighed. "I don't suppose you know him?"

Malcolm shrugged. He was friends with both Nasir and Pierce. But since Malcolm wasn't particularly fond of the blustering fool sitting across from him, there was no chance that he would offer the man an introduction. "We've crossed paths," was all Malcolm would confirm.

Besides, his attention was focused on the third member of the trio sitting at the table by the window. The sunshine glinted off Ella's blonde hair, shoots of gold sparkling around her head and creating almost a halo effect as she sat down. Queen Cassandra was lovely as well and Naya Danilov was a beauty, to be sure. But neither of them were as stunningly gorgeous as Ella. There was just something about her that drew his eye and captured his attention. There was an undefined quality about her that was just...alluring. Perhaps it was the energy that seemed to emanate from her. Or maybe it was that their pasts had collided one too many times over the years. Malcolm wasn't sure. But for the rest of the meal, he was distracted by Ella's beauty and irritated with the pointless ramblings of his pretentious lunch companion.

Finally, the end of the meal arrived and both men stood up. If Malcolm's eyes again drifted towards the three lovely ladies sitting in the corner, he could be excused for his curiosity since most of the other patrons were glancing in that direction as well.

"My lord," his companion stood, bowing slightly. "It has been a pleasure. Please convey my greetings to your father. He doesn't get into the city as often as he used to, does he?"

Malcolm's good humor faded at the mention of his father. "No."

The other man waited for more. Perhaps more of an explanation for the duke's continued absence from society functions or maybe something about his father's health. But Malcolm didn't say a word. A moment later, the man awkwardly nodded, as if understanding the unspoken message, then turned and exited the dining room.

Malcolm made a mental note to call in the irritating man's debts. The lunch had theoretically been a way for the man to obtain an extension on the amount due to Malcolm's company. The man had explained how his factory was doing extremely well and that he had several orders that he hadn't been able to fill because of a lack of capital to expand the business. But what the man had actually revealed was that he had run his business into the ground and probably all that was left was the shell of a factory and a team of disgruntled employees. Since Malcolm had anticipated this, had even loaned him the money so that he would go further into debt, there wasn't an issue. Malcolm could now step in and take over the factory. Exactly as he'd expected. The pompous ass had no idea how to run a manufacturing plant and had spent the loan amount repairing his decaying house and paying for the flighty spending habits of a mistress more than thirty years his junior. A very expensive mistress, Malcolm thought.

And on the subject of women...Malcolm shot another glance at the lovely blond. Time to rekindle an old acquaintance, he decided as he stood and moved across the dining room, weaving his way through the other diners. Malcolm heard his name called by several voices, but he barely acknowledged the calls, intent on one lovely blond with sparkling brown eyes.

From the fury in those gorgeous eyes, Malcolm realized two things; her hatred of him hadn't dimmed over the past decade-plus and...Ella

Fleming was even more stunning close up.

Ella had known that Malcolm Reynolds, Marquis of Theeds, was in the restaurant from the moment she'd entered. There were few who wouldn't notice the tall, shockingly handsome man. His dark hair and cobalt blue eyes were a startling contrast against his tanned skin, revealing a trace of an Irish ancestor in his family's past. But there was something more about him. Something that she couldn't quite put her finger on. Perhaps it was the irritating confidence that always seemed to surround him. Or maybe it was just his height and that hard jawline. The blue eyes that she thought she could see even from across the room?

Whatever it was, Ella had not only seen her family's nemesis, but she'd tracked him as he made his way through the dining room towards her. It was almost as if she could hear his deep, smooth voice over the low hum of conversation from the other diners, even from a distance. He was a powerful person within the global financial world. One of the *most* powerful, she thought. Ella wasn't sure how that had happened since his father's ducal estate was a mess. How had Malcolm gone from the tall, athletic teenager she'd known so many years ago, to the powerfully handsome, confident man in front of her? She didn't know and she had to remind herself that she didn't care!

"Good afternoon, Ella," he said, his smooth, sexy voice sliding over the table. Naya and Cassy smiled politely, doing their political thing. But Ella wasn't married to a global political or financial leader. She didn't have to be polite or diplomatic.

"Go *away*, Malcolm," she replied without prefacing her comment with pleasantries. She hated him with an acidic rage that was unlike anything she'd experienced in her life. And that hatred was justified.

Her poor mother!

Okay, Malcolm hadn't actually killed her mother. He hadn't pulled the trigger or slipped poison into her mother's afternoon tea. But Betty, Ella's mother, had been the housekeeper for the Duke of Theed's estate for twenty years. For twenty years, Ella's beautiful mother had cooked and cleaned for the disgusting Duke of Theeds, Malcolm's father. Her family had lived in the small village just outside of the estate and, at the first sign of sickness, that horrible, disgusting Duke of Theeds, Edward Reynolds, had fired Ella's mother. Thankfully, health coverage in Great Britain wasn't an issue. It was just the demeaning and horrible way that Ella's mother had been kicked to the curb.

Ella had hated him ever since. That's why Ella sat back, watching and observing. Planning. Plotting! She looked on objectively as Malcolm charmed both Naya and Cassy, laughing at their comments and debating various issues. He truly was a handsome man, no doubt about it.

What he didn't know was that Ella knew about a dark mystery that involved Malcolm's family. Something was going on inside his father's estate, something deeply dangerous and evil. Ella knew it and she'd come home to prove it. Malcolm Reynolds, Marquis of Theeds and Edward Reynolds, Duke of Theeds, were going down! She wasn't sure what they were doing, but Ella was fairly sure that it was illegal. She'd come home to prove it and bring their malicious deeds out into the light.

"Good afternoon, ladies," he said with a charming smile, turning his head away from Ella, but he moved his tall, muscular body closer to her.

Naya and Cassy were too polite to ignore him. "Hello, my lord. It's wonderful to see you again," Naya replied. "How is your father these days?"

Ella gritted her teeth, wishing that Naya wasn't so polite.

"He's at home," Malcolm replied, bowing slightly but Ella saw something in his eyes. Had he just closed down? Was there bad blood between father and son? Interesting, she thought.

"Ella, how are you?"

Ella wanted to ignore the man. Her rudeness should have warned him not to speak to her. But before she could reply, Ella remembered the old adage about "attracting more flies with honey than vinegar". So instead of snarling at him, she pulled up the corners of her mouth into what she hoped was a polite smile, even if her eyes didn't convey the same message. "I'm fine, my lord," she replied, although her throat convulsed around the words.

"And how is your father?" he asked, continuing with the ridiculous charade.

Again, she nodded, pulling her smile brighter even as her eyes narrowed. Was that amusement in his blue eyes? "Fine," she replied with a tilt of her head.

He chuckled softly and Ella ignored the tightening of her stomach at the sound. "Good to hear. Why don't you stop by my office some time? We could catch up."

She nodded, thinking he was playing right into her hands. Into the lion's den, she thought! "I might just do that." Although, mentally, she added on the possibility of finding clues about his dark deeds during that "catch up" meeting.

"Good. I look forward to seeing you again," he said, then looked at the two other ladies and nodded. "Ladies," he said to Naya and Cassy, then he turned and walked out of the restaurant.

There was a heavy silence at the table after he left. Ella watched until she couldn't see him any longer, then turned and drained her wine glass in a single gulp, shuddering with fury. "Goodness, I hate that man!" she hissed.

Naya and Cassy chuckled, sipping on their wine. "So *that's* the man, huh?" Cassy commented. "Interesting. He's much more handsome than I would have thought."

Naya nodded. "Yeah, I couldn't see his horns under that head of thick, dark hair. Did you see them pointing out the back?" she asked of Cassy.

Cassy shook her head, straight-faced. "Not a horn in sight."

Ella rolled her eyes. "Right. Aren't you two supposed to be on my side?"

Cassy and Naya laughed, leaning forward. "Absolutely," Cassy replied. "We're here for ya. But he's really is more handsome than I would have thought after what you told us about him back in high school."

Ella toyed with her water glass, contemplating Malcolm and her almost violent reaction to him. "Yes, well, my mother thought he was sweet and adorable, up until the day that his father kicked her out of his house and out of a job."

"But that wasn't the son's fault," Naya pointed out. "You said he was rarely around. So how can you blame the son for the father's sins?"

Ella pressed her lips together. "You know that the duke fired my mother as soon as he found out that she had breast cancer, but that wasn't all that was going on in that house."

"You mentioned something about wild parties," Cassy replied, leaning forward, both of them eager to hear a mystery.

Ella nodded slowly, her eyes narrowing as she glanced at the doors where the man had disappeared. "We never knew what those parties were about," she explained. "But one thing I didn't tell you –because I didn't think it was relevant back then– was that my mother found a small pin, the sort of thing that a man would wear on his lapel."

Her friends leaned forward, their eyes full of curiosity. "One of those small, round pins?" Naya asked, tucking her dark, curls impatiently behind one ear.

"Exactly. At the time, my mother didn't think anything of it. She'd just put it into the pocket of her apron and continued cleaning up. She'd found it right after one of the duke's big, super-secret parties and it was behind one of the heavy chairs in his study. She accidentally brought it home that night but put it on the counter to remind herself to return it the next day."

"Ooh, I'm sensing a mystery here!" Cassy scooted forward on her elbows. "What did the pin look like?"

Ella tilted her head slightly, picturing the pin in her mind. "It was a brass or gold pin with the image of a hand with a flame coming out of the open palm."

Naya nodded eagerly. "Okay, so...what did it represent?"

Ella sighed, twisting her water glass slightly. "I don't know. But when I was in Africa doing that story on teens and pregnancy..."

"The one that got you a Gemstone Award?" Cassy asked.

Ella shrugged and waved her hand impatiently, dismissing the award. "Yeah, but..."

Naya laughed, elbowing Cassy. "Don't you love the way she shrugs off one of the most coveted awards in journalism? Every reporter all over the world would love to win a Gemstone and yet, our Ella just shrugs the award off, as if it were a pointless trophy."

Cassy nodded, grinning as they both stared at their long-time friend. "She probably doesn't even display it."

Cassy and Naya turned to look at Ella who immediately blushed. "Okay, so it *might* be stuffed into a box somewhere," she admitted. "I haven't unpacked from my last move yet."

Cassy rolled her eyes. "You moved two years ago!"

"In her defense, she's rarely home," Naya pointed out. "Not all of us can be globe trotters."

Ella snorted. "Hardly. I travel, but just so that I can do my job." And yet, after several years of living out of a duffel bag, Ella had to admit that the idea of staying in one place for a while held some appeal.

As soon as that thought occurred, she banished it. She was a reporter and had to go where the stories were. Ella worked hard to help people understand how an injustice that was happening in one area of the world was relevant to the rest of the world. Everyone needed to help resolve these issues. So far, her stories had helped small towns all over the world build bridges, schools, doctor's offices, and police forces. By bringing the needs of one small corner of the globe to international attention, Ella had seen wonderful things happen.

She'd also seen horrible things, like tragic, devastating wars and desperate starvation caused by merciless despots. She'd seen people and animals dying due to dehydration after a ruler disrupted waterways, causing impossible cruelty and environmental devastation. But she'd also seen strangers pull together to battle those brutal forces. She'd seen miracles happen when people became aware of an injustice in the world. And she'd seen villages rise up against a seemingly impenetrable force – all because they knew that something or someone had to be stopped, changed, or fixed.

So no, Ella couldn't stay in one place. She loved traveling and making a difference in the world. Ella was good at her job and it renewed her faith in humanity. Her job was her identity and it was what made her get up every morning with excitement and purpose.

"I am so proud of everything that you write," Cassy said, lifting her hand to call the waiter. "But right now, I think we need dessert. I haven't had dessert in months! And I miss our late night ice cream binges."

Ella laughed and clapped her hands. "Everything?" she asked, her eyes sparkling as she looked at her two friends.

Naya grinned, nodding fervently. "Absolutely! We ordered salads for lunch!"

The waiter arrived, looking delightfully solicitous. "Are you ladies ready for the check?"

Cassy laughed and looked up at the waiter. "We'd like everything on your dessert menu," she told him.

The waiter looked stumped for a moment. "You'd like to look at the dessert menu?" he offered.

Ella shook her head, offering a grin that transformed her features. In a flash, Ella changed from a serious but beautiful woman, to a mischievous elf, eyes sparkling and her up-tilted nose squinching slightly. "No, we'd like to order one of everything on the dessert menu, please."

The waiter included each of the ladies in a confused stare. Obviously, no one had ever ordered every dessert the restaurant offered before. But for Naya, Ella, and Cassy, this was a tradition. They were good about their eating habits most of the time. But when they got together, they didn't care about calories. They loved having a bit of freedom from the stress of their regular lives. Ordering decadent desserts was a small rebellion against the decorum their lives normally required.

The waiter snapped his mouth closed, then nodded and bowed. "Right away, ladies," and he smiled as he walked away to put in their order.

For the next hour, they laughed and dined on elaborate, decadent desserts that included a citrus mousse topped with candied lemon spirals and lemon cream, a peppermint and chocolate cake with candied frosting, brown sugar caramel pound cake, peanut butter and chocolate pie, and a pear and almond tort. By the time the three of them scraped away the last of the cream and finished off another bottle of white wine, they were laughing as they recalled some of their high school pranks. It was one of the most relaxing afternoons Ella had enjoyed in a long time!

Chapter 2

"Dad?!" Ella called out as she entered her father's cottage, dumping her messenger bag by the front door.

Silence. "Outside," she muttered, smiling in anticipation of finding her father in his garden. Tom Fleming loved to garden and had the most beautiful tulips in the spring, the largest and most vibrant hydrangeas and, in late summer, the most glorious roses. He worked at the post office in the mornings, taking the early shift so that he could be home by mid-afternoon to work in his garden. Ella's father barely took the time to take off his postal uniform before he shuffled off to get gardening. Tom Fleming cooked and cleaned his neat cottage on the edge of the village, but his garden was truly his pride and joy.

When there was still silence, Ella called out again, opening the back door. Then she paused, breathing in the scents of orange and lilac. "Oh my!"

"Ella!" her father called, poking his head up from behind one of the rose bushes. "You're home!" and he pushed his hat back on his head as he shuffled out from behind the bushes. With open arms, he hurried over to Ella, wrapping her into a hug that was warm and reassuring. "Oh, it's good to see you!" he gushed. Pulling back, he looked down into her eyes, his fatherly gaze making sure that she was whole and healthy. "You look wonderful, honey," he told her sincerely.

"So do you, Dad," she returned his hug with interest. "I missed you!"

He laughed and threw an arm over her shoulder. "I missed you too! Tell me where you've been over the past few weeks. I lost track of you when you headed out to Mozambique."

They settled in the kitchen with the ancient appliances that still worked due to her father's ability to fix any and everything. If it had an engine, he could make it purr like a kitten. He grabbed a pitcher of iced tea and poured them tall glasses, then sat down at the beaten kitchen table to listen and talk. They laughed about her travels and his garden while Ella felt the tension ease out of her shoulders.

"I saw Malcolm Reynolds yesterday," she said, after taking a long swallow of her iced tea.

"You saw his lordship?" Tom asked, none of the animosity in his voice that Ella had conveyed yesterday. "How is he?"

She shrugged, nibbling a cookie. "Pompous as ever. He interrupted my lunch with Cassy and Naya."

His furry eyebrows lowered. "Now, Ella, that doesn't sound very polite," he admonished, topping off their glasses. "Besides, he's a lord. You should treat him with respect."

Ella laughed softly, shaking her head. "Right. Not gonna happen, Dad. His family treated Mom horribly. I am only returning the favor."

Tom sighed heavily. "How are your friends?" he asked, changing the subject. "I see their pictures in the papers occasionally. They become more beautiful every year."

Ella smiled, ignoring the pinch of jealousy at the thought of her friends' happiness. "They're doing really well," she replied.

"Do you ever hear from those other three girls from high school?" he asked. "What were their names? Tamara and...?"

Ella groaned. "We were just talking about them yesterday. And no," she grimaced. "I don't hear from Tamara, Willow, or Lana. Why would I? We might have lived across the hallway from each other, but we weren't really friends. Acquaintances at best."

Tom shook his head. "I never understood why. It seemed as if all of you girls had something in common. I remember meeting them during parent's week and they seemed nice."

"They came from a different background, Dad," Ella explained, even though she'd explained this several times to her father. "They were all incredibly wealthy and could buy just about anything they wanted. What could we have had in common?"

"Seems like your commonality was school and living so far away from your families, but maybe that's just me." He stood up and started taking food out of the fridge to make dinner for the two of them. "So, what are you working on now? Any deep mystery happening out in the world?"

This was a subject she felt more comfortable talking about. "Yes!" she said eagerly. "Remember when Mom came home from cleaning the house after those big, secret parties on the estate?" she asked.

"Sure!" he chuckled. "Nothing irritated your mother more than not knowing what was going on. She loved walking through the neighborhoods at night in the fall, so she could see into everyone's windows."

Ella laughed at the memory, relieved that it didn't hurt anymore to think of her mother. Instead, there was simply a soft, warm feeling. "Well, I remember one time she showed me a small, gold pin, the kind that men wear on their lapels."

Her father tilted his head slightly, thinking back to that day. A moment later, he nodded as he spread mustard on fresh bread. "I remember that. Something about a hand and..." he shook his head. "I can't remember what else. But she talked about it for days after that party, thinking that she'd stumbled onto a secret society or something."

Ella's eyes sharpened as the spark of curiosity leapt up inside of her. "A flame coming out of the palm of the hand."

"Right!" he said, pointing the mustard-covered knife in the air. "That was it. Okay, so what about it?"

"Well, I was in a village in Tular recently," she explained, leaning forward. "Several of the women had disappeared one night. When I started asking questions, a witness said that they remembered seeing a stranger wearing a shirt with an emblem on the right corner. A hand with a flame coming out of the palm." She waited for her father to understand the significance.

He stopped making sandwiches and turned to look at Ella. "You think there's a connection between a party an old man had more than fifteen years ago and someone walking by a village in another continent?" he asked incredulously.

Ella shrugged and accepted the sandwich he offered. "I don't know. But I'm going to find out."

Tom sighed and took his seat across from her again. "If Edward Reynolds is involved, it might be dangerous, honey."

Ella took a sip of her lemonade. "I don't care. If that man is doing something illegal, I'm going to find out."

Her father's eyes turned wary. "What if the man just had a party with weird, kinky sex?"

Ella cringed. "Eww! That's too horrible to think about." She put her sandwich down, not really hungry anyway. "It's possible that he had some kinky sex parties, Dad. But what if he had a party with women who weren't there voluntarily?" she offered. "What if that man is involved in sex trafficking?"

Her father's eyes sharpened now, anger starting to burn inside of him. "You think it's something that nefarious?"

Ella sighed and looked down at the table, thinking, trying to put the puzzle pieces together, but there were too many holes. "I won't know until I look into the issue. There's definitely a connection. That pin and the description of the symbol on the shirt...they're too similar. And the women who had disappeared, they were sick and vulnerable. Two had been kidnapped the month before, beaten brutally, and weren't recovering well. They needed medical attention, the kind that the small villagers couldn't provide."

"That' sounds awful," Tom replied with a heavy sigh. "I know that you dive into these mysteries and, so far, you've come out unscathed. But Ella, please be careful with this one. If there is a connection to Edward Reynolds and the disappearing women, then..."

Ella put her hand on her father's forearm. "I'll be careful," she promised. "I've learned over the years to be discreet."

Tom sighed, nodding but he didn't pick up his sandwich again. "Good," he told her. "Good."

Chapter 3

"Figures," Ella grumbled, staring up at the imposing building that housed the headquarters of Reynolds Industries. Over the past few days, she'd done her research and, although the Duke of Theeds, Edward Reynolds, was still alive, he wasn't active in the social world anymore. But he hadn't passed his title or wealth on to his son, Malcolm Reynolds. In a way, Ella respected Malcolm more because he'd created so much from nothing. He hadn't inherited his wealth, like so many rich aristocrats in the world. He'd created a massive empire through grit and determination. He was thirty-six years old and a billionaire many times over. He bought ailing companies, fixed them up, and sold them off. So he didn't really own anything, other than a huge amount of land and real estate, all of which was separate from his investment company.

And yet, she remembered that shiver of awareness a couple of days ago at the restaurant. The man was tall and arrogant, she thought. But if there was one thing that had never impressed her, it was wealth. In fact, because of the way Edward Reynolds had treated Ella's mother, the way the arrogant jerk had simply tossed her out of his house because he could, his disdain for decades of loyalty and service had caused Ella to despise people with a disproportionate amount of wealth. They had too much power and, in most cases, wielded that power with contemptuous disregard for anyone outside of their social circle.

But staring up at this imposing building, Ella felt...something. Something strange that...well, it wasn't important, she thought. "He's just compensating," she muttered.

"What do you suspect I'm compensating for?" a deep voice asked from behind her.

Startled, Ella swung around, finding Malcolm Reynolds much closer than she'd anticipated. Much closer and...had he grown a few inches taller over the past few days? The man was crazy tall! Well over six feet. Ella was five feet, seven inches, so she was relatively tall for a woman. Plus she'd worn black boots with three inch heels. But good grief! Malcolm Reynolds still towered over her!

"What are you doing out here?" she gasped, stepping back to put some space between them.

Those cobalt blue eyes sparkled with amusement, the corners crinkling enticingly. "Am I not supposed to be outside?"

Her eyes narrowed as she realized that he was teasing her. "You're supposed to be inside, destroying people's lives," she retorted with a defiant lift of her chin.

"Ah," he laughed, leaning back slightly. "Well, I broke up ten families this morning, so I thought I'd take a break. Would you like to come inside?" he offered. "We can throw a dart on the wall and see who I should destroy this afternoon. Would be fun...."

Ella bristled at his tone. "This is funny to you?" she demanded, her temper increasing with his mocking attitude.

"A little," he replied with a soft chuckle, putting a hand to the small of her back as he led her into the building. "I think that you are a brilliant reporter, Ella. I've followed your career over the years and I've been impressed with not only by your bravery at reporting on horrible situations, but also your talent at conveying those issues."

He pressed a button on the elevator and, almost immediately, the elevator appeared. With that hand still at her back, he nudged her into the elevator and they rose. Since this was a glass elevator that looked out at the city, Ella automatically stepped away from the glass and the scary heights. Unfortunately, she stepped back...against him. For a stolen instant, she could feel the hard muscles of his chest against her back and his strong arms around her waist. It was a shocking but intensely pleasant sensation and, since it had been a long time since she'd even kissed a man, it took her a moment to pull away.

"Sorry," she muttered, jerking away from him. But she didn't move too far. The glass of the elevator might be thick, but she didn't trust anything to keep her safe this high above the ground. Unfortunately, that left her standing awkwardly in the middle of the elevator and she almost jumped through the doors when they finally opened on the executive floor.

Breathing deeply, she looked around, trying to calm her racing nerves. Obviously, Ella wasn't a huge fan of heights and she looked up at Malcolm, bracing herself for his amusement at her expense.

"This way," he said and gestured towards one end of the elegantly decorated hallway. No jokes about her fear of heights, no pity or laughter in his eyes? Ella was confused because...he *wasn't* going to laugh at her?

Reluctantly grateful, Ella followed him down the elegantly decorated hallway, looking around, trying to take in everything as she passed.

Feelings, smells, other people's expressions. Everything would be included in her story.

Malcolm paused at an older woman's desk. "Nancy, would you order some lunch for us? We're going to be a while."

Ella frowned. "I'm not staying for lunch," she told him, even though she was famished. She'd skipped breakfast this morning, wanting to check in with her editor before coming to meet with Malcolm.

Nancy ignored Ella and nodded to her boss before turning back to her computer. Order lunch online? That would be excellent! Ella had been out of the country for so long, living in mud huts, tin-roofed houses, or tents...none of which had had reliable internet service. She'd read articles about these conveniences, but since she'd only been back in London for a few days, she hadn't experienced the glory of ordering food from one's phone and having it delivered, hot and yummy, to one's doorstep. Her idea of convenience over the past few years was picking ripe fruit from a tree.

Ella tore her curious eyes away from Nancy's computer and hurried after Malcolm into the office.

"Close the door," Malcolm ordered.

Ella had to restrain herself from slamming it while curtsying. Sarcastically, of course. But she stepped back and quietly closed the door, then turned to face the man she was going to put into prison.

"So..."

"I read that story you did on last month on human trafficking. It was brilliant. Do you think it will do any good?"

Ella had written about the desperate situation in several countries, which created an environment where teenage girls could be enticed to apply for "jobs" in other countries. Unfortunately, the modeling jobs, nanny positions, and housekeeping roles never materialized. Instead, those vulnerable girls were forced into horrible situations, beaten and drugged, sold off as prostitutes, and never seen by their families again. Most of them died and were simply tossed into the streets or a pit somewhere out of the way, easily replaced by yet another girl trying desperately to "make it" in the world.

"I don't know. I ensured that the articles also ran in the smaller newspapers. So if the article saves even one girl from being kidnapped and used, then that's a good thing."

He nodded sharply, those cobalt blue eyes sharp and intelligent. "I agree. What are you working on now?"

She smiled, sitting down in the club chair across from him. "I've come across some interesting leads for a story that, I suspect, started decades ago. Maybe longer."

"I'm intrigued." He opened his mouth to say more, but a knock sounded and Nancy stepped into the office carrying a full tray of food and drinks. "Thank you, Nancy," Malcolm said and she smiled, set the tray down onto the table between them and walked out quietly, pulling the door closed behind her.

"Please, help yourself," he said, referring to the tray of small sandwiches. There were small plates and fruit along with sodas.

"I'm fine," Ella replied, waving the food away.

"Do you mind if I go ahead? I've been in meetings since early this morning and I'm starving."

Ella shrugged. "Fine by me," she told him, then watched, fascinated as he put several of the small sandwiches onto a plate.

"You were telling me about your next revelation?" he prompted.

"I'm working on putting you and your rich cronies into prison," she announced.

That got a smile out of him and Ella wondered about it. Was he so confident about his social status as an aristocrat that he thought of himself as immune to conviction? Or was he innocent of whatever was going on with the secret society?

"That is really going to put a dent in my social life," he chuckled. "What do you think I've done to warrant a prison sentence?' he asked, leaning back and taking another bite of his sandwich.

Ella watched him, oddly fascinated by his hands. They were strong, with long, deft fingers. What was it about those hands was so interesting?

She jerked her eyes away from his hands and looked up at his features. "Um..." focus! "Have you ever heard or seen a symbol like this one?" she asked, pulling out her notebook and flipping to the page where she'd sketched the flaming hand symbol.

Malcolm leaned forward, his eyes looking over the picture before leaning back. "What does it mean?" he asked.

Ella noticed that he hadn't answered her question. Interesting, she thought. "I don't know what it means. Yet," she paused significantly. "But I'm going to find out, Malcolm."

"Where did you first see that symbol?" he asked.

She shook her head. "Doesn't matter. But what do you know about it?"

"Oh, I'm sure that there are secret societies all over the world, Ella."

She smiled triumphantly. "Another evasive answer."

He laughed and Ella ignored the jump in her stomach at the deep, rich sound. "You're not giving me a whole lot to go on. Perhaps if you tell me when you saw the symbol, I might be able to help you a bit more."

She shook her head. "I don't give out my sources, Malcolm. You should know that, being in business and all."

"Being in business isn't nearly as mysterious as investigating crimes, I suspect."

Ella tilted her head, fascinated by his answer. "I would have thought that our jobs were pretty similar. I find out a small bit of information, a thread of mystery. I keep tugging on that thread, discovering those mysteries and bring them to light. In your line of business, you find a clue that a previously strong company has been mismanaged, am I right?" she asked.

"I hunt down companies that are struggling financially," he confirmed.

"And then you keep tugging, looking at data and financial records, checking on the company's sales and stock values."

"You've done your research well," he replied, setting the now-empty plate on the table. "And you think that this symbol," he pointed his chin towards her notebook still open on the low coffee table, "involves something nefarious, dark, and evil?" he asked. "This is the string at which you are pulling, looking under rocks and behind the curtains to find out what's going on."

She stood up, feeling the need to get away from his distractingly handsome smile. "I'm going to find out what this means, Malcolm," she warned, stuffing her notebook back into her messenger bag. "And I'm going to treat you exactly as you treated my mother when she told your family that she was sick."

He'd stood as well, moving closer to her. "I'm very sorry about what my father did to your mother," he said.

Ella jerked, startled by his words. Looking up into those blue eyes, she felt...something strange again.

Pulling back, she blinked and stepped away from the chair. "Right. Well, it's in the past."

"Is it?" he asked gently. "I remember the day that my mother passed away." His jaw clenched and he shook his head slightly. "My father announced that she'd passed and that the funeral was in three days. He ordered me to wear my dark suit." Malcolm's hands slid into his pockets. "I don't think one ever truly gets over the death of a parent, do we?"

Was he closer now? Ella realized that she'd been staring up into his eyes and hadn't noticed him walking towards her.

"It was...years ago." And yet, she could still remember holding her mother's hand in the hospital, seeing the pain in her eyes as the cancer slowly destroyed her.

Malcolm reached out, brushing a light finger down over her cheek.

The touch both burned and soothed...it short-circuited her brain.

"You're quite lovely, Ella," he murmured, almost as if he were talking to himself.

Startled, she looked up into his blue eyes, not sure what to say. Never in her wildest imagination would she have expected him to say something like that. Lovely? She wanted to snort with disbelief. Naya was lovely! Cassy! She was a gorgeous woman! Ella knew that she wasn't ugly, but...she wasn't lovely.

But standing here, in front of Malcolm, for some strange reason, she did feel...oddly beautiful. For all her life, she'd pushed to be smart and brave, to confront the injustices in the world. Never had she felt beautiful. This man... his eyes and his electric touch ...caused her to feel pretty.

Why wasn't she leaving? They were standing there, the silence and tension expanding as they stared into each other's eyes. Ella told herself to walk away. But her feet didn't move.

That's when he did something even more astounding.

Ella watched in stunned fascination as he leaned in and kissed her! His lips, so firm and temptingly commanding, brushed over hers, eliciting a startled response from her own. The tingling in her lips was so astonishing that she forgot to pull away. He did it again and again, his lips brushing back and forth against hers and Ella stood there, taking it. No, not just accepting the kiss...her lips actually moved, actually participated in the kiss!

The ache in her belly and the burning sensation against her lips was so new, so strange that she finally pulled away. For another long moment, she just blinked at him, wondering what the hell had just happened!

"Right," she whispered into the silence.

With that, she turned and walked out of his office, feeling stunned and...tingly. And ashamed! She'd just kissed Malcolm Reynolds! What in the world? Why? Why had she simply stood there? Why hadn't she slapped him and given him some pithy set-down that would humiliate him?

Ella stepped into the elevator, too stunned and confused to even fear the glass-enclosed space as it whisked her silently down to the lobby. Down and away from the man she wanted to see in prison.

The man she'd just...kissed!

Malcolm stared at the now-empty doorway, more intrigued than before as he replayed Ella's soft, trembling response to his kiss. Ella was startlingly beautiful, but also tough and sexy with her tight jeans and black boots. Her messenger bag was scruffy and well worn, but was of obvious quality. Her clothes weren't rumpled, as he'd expected. She was...lovely. Her blonde hair was straight and long, shining in the overhead lights. While other women of his acquaintance would have done something to bring his attention to their long hair, flipping it over their shoulder or twirling a lock around their fingers...Ella's hair was brushed but forgotten.

She wore minimal makeup, just a touch of mascara and lipstick. Her skin was soft and creamy, making her appear youthful and strong. She was a capable woman wrapped up in soft femininity that, Malcolm suspected, the lovely Ella tried hard to hide and ignore.

An impossible task, he thought with a chuckle as he stood and walked to his desk. Ella couldn't hide her beauty any more than she could ignore a mystery. It was all part of her lovely package and...he was determined to get to know her better. Ella Fleming had always intrigued him. But now, with maturity and bright determination, she got to him in different ways. She was more than simply a curiosity.

She was a challenge!

Damn, she was beautiful! And smart and didn't give an inch! He liked that about her.

What he didn't like was that she might be getting close to something that he and his friends had been working on for the past several years.

Picking up his phone, he dialed a number. "Jenna," he replied as soon as his friend answered. "I just spoke with Ella Fleming and, apparently, she's onto us." He paused, listening. "Right. But we need to be a bit more discreet. Otherwise, the whole operation could be revealed, which would put our people in danger."

Hanging up, he wondered if...was his father still countering the group's efforts? Were his father and his cronies still active? Malcolm had thought that their efforts had been shut down, but perhaps it was time to make sure.

Chapter 4

Ella paced the confines of her tiny apartment. The whole place was really just two rooms – a combined kitchen and den area and her bedroom. Okay, maybe three rooms because she had a bathroom too. But do bathrooms really count as a separate room? Probably not. And why in the world was she debating the number of rooms in her apartment?

Because she didn't want to face up to the issue that was really bothering her. Which was that she couldn't understand why she'd reacted so intensely to Malcolm's kiss today. Good grief, they'd argued...and she'd...!

Ella dropped onto her sofa, holding her head in her hands. "What in the world happened today?" she muttered. Throughout their conversation, she'd been distracted by his hands, his mouth, his eyes...just about every part of him. Then when they'd stood by the door...something had just snapped inside of her. So she hadn't been able to resist when he'd lowered his head and...kissed her!

"It was crazy! Just an insane moment in time," she said out loud. Unfortunately, there wasn't anyone in her apartment to tell her that she was wrong.

"I need pictures," she decided, looking at the blank walls. There was a sofa against one wall and she had some utensils in the drawers of her kitchen. A bed in her bedroom with sheets and a blanket along with several pillows. Shampoo in her bathroom, but other than that, she had nothing. Oh, she had a large bank balance. Her success over the years and her lack of expenses, lack of spending, had helped her grow her bank balance into a respectable amount.

"I really should decorate," she told herself. "Maybe if I added a bit of color here and there, I wouldn't stay away so long."

She stopped and looked around, startled by those words. "Stick around? Why in the world would I want to stay here?" she muttered. "The stories are out in the world! That's what I do! I go out and find injustices in the world and tell everyone about them."

Ella sighed and leaned back against the cushions of the sofa. "And still, not the issue that I should be facing at the moment." Getting up, she walked into her kitchen, needing a beer or a glass of wine, something that would help her relax so that she wasn't wound up so tightly. Unfortunately, she'd only been back home for a few days. She didn't even have food in her fridge yet. Good grief, she hadn't even *turned on* her fridge! Because she was gone for so many months at a time, she turned off the fridge and even unplugged it in order to save energy. Ella had been in too many places around the world that didn't have electricity, so there was no way that she'd take it for granted or waste it when she wasn't even around to enjoy it.

"I'm doing it again," she laughed, shaking her head as she pushed the fridge door closed. "Okay, so I kissed him. That's not a crime. A simple kiss isn't going to skew my perspective at all!" Ella looked around, but the sofa didn't agree with her. "It won't!"

She sighed and shifted on her feet. "I'm really getting antsy if I'm talking to the sofa." Grabbing her messenger bag and her keys, she pulled the bag's strap over her shoulder. "I know exactly how I can move on. I'm going to find evidence that he's involved!"

Leaving her apartment, she rushed down the stairs and jumped into her car. It was a tiny hatchback that didn't take up much space or use a lot of gas. It was also easy to maneuver around the crowded city streets.

At this time of the night, there weren't many cars around. It was the perfect time to do a bit of snooping, she told herself with a secret smile. It took her about a half hour to get out of the city. Heading towards the warehouse district, she looked around, glanced at the information she'd logged into her notebook and easily found the right warehouse.

Parking several blocks away, she stepped out of her car and looked around. It wasn't the safest neighborhood in the world, but it wasn't the worst she'd ever been in either. She pulled a wool cap out of her bag, tugging it down over her hair and tucking all of the blond strands underneath. She'd learned over the years that it was better not to be too obviously feminine when sneaking around in dangerous parts of the world.

She pulled open her bag again and checked her supplies. Flashlight, cell phone, extra batteries, Taser...everything was there along with her notebook and pens. She loved her job!

She slipped along the streets, keeping close to the buildings and aware of her surroundings. Thankfully, she made it to the right warehouse without running into anyone. Checking the door, she realized that it was locked with a magnetic lock and keypad. "Darn it!" she whispered. Can't pick that lock, she thought as she bit down on her lower lip, her mind working to come up with an alternative plan. Stepping back, she scanned the building. There were windows, but they were all pretty high up. Walking around the building, she smiled when she spotted the dumpsters pushed up against one wall. The area around the warehouse was surprisingly tidy, and the dumpsters would help her reach the window right above it. Hopefully, the window wasn't locked.

"Sir," a big, tall man stepped into Malcolm's office. "I'm sorry to disturb you so late at night, but there's been a break-in at the warehouse."

Malcolm turned and looked at the man. "At the warehouse? Why would anyone break in there? Everything is secured..." as soon as he spoke, the image of a gorgeous blonde woman popped into his mind. "Right," he replied.

"I have video, sir. We're tracking the person and..."

"Let me see it," he grumbled and reached for the tablet. As soon as he focused on the figure, who was dangling by her fingertips from the balcony above the main floor of the warehouse, Malcolm knew it was Ella. He'd know that figure anywhere. Even as he watched her, Malcolm acknowledged that she looked hot in the black jeans and black jacket. Unfortunately, all of that blonde hair was tucked away underneath a cap, but he still recognized her.

"This is Ella Fleming," Malcolm told his head of security. "She thinks that I'm involved in a secret society."

John smiled. "The flaming hand?"

"Yeah, how'd you know?"

John chuckled. "She asked me about it yesterday. I didn't tell her anything, sir."

"Good. She's not ready for the information yet. But eventually, I suspect that we'll have to let her in on the plan."

John nodded in agreement. "Just tell me when, sir."

"Soon," Malcolm replied with a heavy sigh, rubbing his forehead. "In the meantime," he looked at the image on the tablet, "Let's get her out of there. There's nothing except machine parts. But still, that's a dangerous..." he stopped when the tablet picked up another person. "There's someone else in the warehouse!"

John turned the tablet, his sharp eyes taking in the various images on the screen. "That's not one of our men, sir. I don't recognize him."

"Ella is in danger!" he growled. A moment later, he was out the door, racing down the stairs because the elevator would take too long.

It took less than five minutes to reach the warehouse with Malcolm driving while John was on his phone with his security team and watching the progress of the two people stealthily moving through the warehouse via the video feeds. Each seemed completely unware of the other, but Malcolm wasn't taking any chances. He sped through the nearly empty streets and screeched to a halt just outside the door of the warehouse.

"We need to go in quietly," Malcolm said. "I don't want to scare off the other guy. He might realize that Ella is there and do something stupid."

"Agree," John murmured.

"You go to the left, I'll go to the right," Malcolm ordered. "I'll ping your cell phone if I find her."

"I'll do the same," John silently opened the door to the warehouse, nodding when they both stepped inside.

Malcolm knew the direction Ella was heading and slipped through the piles of crates. Everything was neat and orderly and he moved ahead of where he suspected she was going, watching her on the tablet the whole time. It was eerily quiet within the warehouse and he looked around, wondering briefly where the other guy was. Malcolm focused on getting to Ella. John would take care of the other guy.

He glanced down at the tablet, then up at the aisle markings. Turning left, Malcolm watched when Ella headed right and he moved quickly. When he was finally in position, he tucked himself between two large wooden crates, and waited. Watching the tablet, he held his breath… then reached out. With one hand, he covered her mouth and wrapped his other arm around her waist, pulling her back against his chest between the crates.

She fought wildly, her nails digging into the skin on his forearm. But he gently tightened his hold. "Be quiet, Tiger," he whispered into her ear. "There's someone else in here with you and I don't think he's…" she stopped struggling and they both went very still. A moment later, a tall man dressed in black wearing a ski mask walked by their hiding place. He didn't see them, but he was obviously looking for something. His flashlight came on and the light lit up the wooden crate opposite where the two of them were hiding.

They didn't move until the man walked on, obviously still searching.

A moment later, there was a scuffle and Ella tensed. "It's just my security guy. He'll catch the other guy," he whispered into her ear.

Ella let out her breath slowly and Malcolm felt every muscle in her body press against his. She was tense, but slowly the tension left her and he released her, knowing that she'd be quiet now. Ella leaned back against the wooden crate behind her, staring up at him, but he couldn't see her eyes in the dim light of the warehouse.

"All clear, sir!" his head of security texted to Malcolm.

Malcolm showed her the text and they both relaxed.

"What the hell are you doing in here?" she demanded a moment later.

Malcolm was stunned by her question initially, but after a pregnant moment, he threw back his head, laughing at her audacity. Only Ella could break into a building and then be furious that the owner was there as well. Damn, she was magnificent.

When his laughter was under control, he replied, "I own the building. Mind telling me what you're doing in here? And just as important, how the hell did you get in? The locks to this place are state of the art!"

Ella shrugged. "The locks on your windows aren't though," she replied and he noticed that she didn't explain what she was doing.

"And?" he prompted.

"And what?" she replied as if offended by his question.

Malcom wasn't sure if he wanted to laugh or spank her sexy butt. Both, probably. She deserved both, he thought. Although the second might lead to something more than just a spanking.

And that, he thought, wasn't such a horrible idea.

"Do you have any idea what kind of danger you put yourself into?"

She shifted, almost as if she were bristling for a fight. "Yes. Do you?"

He wanted to laugh again. Instead, he put his hands on her upper arms and shook her. "Ella! You could have been killed!"

"But I *wasn't*!" she pointed out.

He stopped and looked down at her, then took a long, slow, deep breath. "Ella, you could have been hurt."

"Yeah, and you could have been sent to prison," she countered.

He looked down at her, those amazing blue eyes glaring right back up at him and he couldn't help it. He laughed, shaking his head. He laughed so hard, he had to brace his hands on either side of her head. "Damn, woman! No one can spin this situation around like you can."

"Thank you," she muttered with a scowl. "I think."

That only caused him to laugh harder, which was exactly how John found them.

"I'm sorry sir, but my team lost him. He was..." John stopped, looking between the two of them, noticing their positions against the crate. There was curiosity in the man's eyes, but he wisely kept his questions to himself.

"Would you like me to call the police?" John asked.

Malcolm knew that Ella was watching him, daring him to allow the security expert to bring in official help. But he didn't take her bait. If it had been only the other person who had broken into the warehouse, Malcolm definitely would have brought in the authorities. But for some reason, he couldn't allow Ella to be led away in handcuffs.

Not unless he was doing the handcuffing.

"No, that won't be necessary, but see what your team can find out." He started to turn away, then looked back at John. "Discreetly," he warned.

"Yes, sir," the guard replied, then turned away and gathered up his team for a strategy session.

"You're coming with me," Malcolm took her arm, leading her out of the warehouse towards his car. John had driven with him over here, but Malcolm knew John could get back to the headquarters building with one of his team. He wanted Ella alone to interrogate her on whatever the hell she thought she might find in that warehouse.

"What if I don't want to come with you?" she demanded, tugging against his hold.

He stopped and glared down at her. "Then I will call the police and I will press charges for breaking and entering. It's your choice," he told her, his voice low and gravelly.

Ella stared up at the man, startled. "You wouldn't."

"Ella, so help me, don't you dare challenge me! It's late, I'm more turned on than I care to be at this time of the night, we have a ton of unfinished business from earlier today, and I'm ready to spank your adorable ass. But if you challenge me, I'm perfectly fine with calling the police and having them arrest you. Because if I do, at least I'll know that you are safe for the night."

She'd never seen him like this before. Ella remembered him from her childhood, watching him ride his horse through the pastures of his father's estate or laughing with his friends as they walked through the village. He always looked so cool and in control. Even earlier this afternoon, when she'd been losing her mind to his touch, he'd appeared to be completely unaffected. Turned on, but not out of control. That had pissed her off more than she'd realized until just now. But seeing him lose it like this seemed to ease her own tension.

"Fine," she replied, lifting her chin. It was a dare, but she couldn't help it. He just...there was something about him that tormented her, kept her from simply acquiescing to his authority. Sure, she'd just violated the law, possibly several laws, by breaking into his warehouse. But she couldn't simply bow down to him. She still suspected him of being an international criminal.

So, why did she kind of like the idea of him spanking her? Why did the idea turn her on to the point where she was more than a little...crazy? With need! None of this made any sense. And since it was Ella's job to make sense of the world and report her findings, she felt as if she were losing the threads of her life's goal. Of her mind, even!

"Get into the car, Ella!" he snapped.

She hesitated for a moment, but in the end, she didn't have much choice. He simply scooped her up and deposited her into the passenger seat.

Ella stayed, but only because she was fascinated by this darker side of Malcolm. At least, that's what she told herself. That explanation was good enough for the moment. Later, she'd go through the events of the night, as well as her reactions, and hopefully figure out what was really going on.

Chaos! Craziness! Ella sat in the passenger seat as Malcolm drove through the quiet streets back to his headquarters. She wanted to tell him to just let her off at the corner, but she seriously doubted that he'd let her get away that easily. Not until he had answers.

When he pulled into the reserved parking space in his building, he got out and came around to the other side, politely opening the passenger door for her. Ella sat there for a long moment, thinking it was strange that some women waited for men to open their doors. Where had that custom come from? Was there a point in history when women's hands had simply fallen off? Or was there some other reason why women waited for men to open doors for them.

"Ella?"

She jerked at the sharp snap of his voice. "Fine! I'm getting out! No need to get snippy."

He sighed as soon as she stepped out of the vehicle, then closed the door after her. "This way," he ordered, but didn't wait for her to follow his command. He put a hand on her upper arm and forcibly led her over to the elevators. It opened immediately and they stepped inside.

Unfortunately, the intimacy of the quiet elevator didn't help her state of mind. The tension increased until Ella couldn't take it any longer. One moment, she was standing next to him, literally feeling the heat coming from his tall, muscular body, and the next moment, she was in the corner.

He turned and looked at her, one dark eyebrow lifted in question.

She lifted a shoulder. "You're just...hot."

He chuckled. "Thank you."

Ella rolled her eyes, ignoring the blush that stole up her cheeks. "Not hot, as in attractive," she told him, although he definitely was! Attractive, that is. "You're hot as in it is uncomfortable to stand next to you."

"Right." He nodded, obviously not believing her. He stepped closer, trapping her against the corner of the elevator. "We're going to get to the bottom of this."

Ella glared up at him defiantly. "I'm not telling you what I was doing in the warehouse.

He smiled, a slow, sexy expression that lit his blue eyes with a dangerous heat. "I wasn't referring to the warehouse. I'm going to find out what you were looking for, Ella. But at the moment, I'm more interested in resolving the tension that caused you to hide in the corner."

The elevator pinged, indicating that they'd reached the executive floor. She sighed with relief, but when he didn't move to exit, she simply grinned up at him...then ducked under his arm and walked out by herself, leaving him alone.

She walked into his office, assuming that's where he wanted to discuss the night's events. Sure enough, he walked in behind her and slammed the office door behind him. "Okay, explain."

Ella's shoulders pulled back and she glared up at him. "What do you want to know?"

He stared at her for a long moment, then sighed, rubbing a hand through his hair. "Ella, it's late, you were almost killed, you broke into a warehouse filled with machinery that's about to be shipped to Malaysia, and...what the hell were you looking for?" he demanded.

"Women," she admitted. "Girls, actually."

He stared at her, not comprehending. "Why would there be any women or girls in that warehouse? Especially at night." He paused, rubbing a hand over the back of his neck. "I know that there are women that work in the warehouse during the day," he offered. "Did one of them... is there something illegal happening with one of my employees? If that's the case, I need to know."

She shook her head. "Not an employee," she told him. "At least, not an official employee. I'm looking for women who were kidnapped and are now being used for sex slaves."

He cringed, pulling back. "That's disgusting!" he lashed out. "Why would...?" he stopped, his back stiffening. "Hell, you think that there are women being trafficked through *my* warehouses?" He moved closer to her, his eyes hard and determined now. "Tell me what you've found. I guarantee that I'll put a stop to it. I'll work with you any way I can."

Ella blinked, stunned by his offer. She eyed him carefully, trying to gauge the sincerity of his words. He certainly looked and sounded earnest, both about his horror that someone was using his warehouse for illegal purposes, as well as his offer to work with the authorities to stop whoever was doing the atrocities.

"You'd be willing to let the police into your warehouse and look around?" she asked, trying to clarify.

"Any time, any place," he confirmed. "If someone is shipping women into the country, or out of it, then I want it stopped. I don't condone illegal activities," he told her firmly. "I know that you don't believe me. So, what can I do to prove it to you?"

She edged closer, looking into his eyes. "I know that you recognized the symbol I showed you earlier today. I could see it in your eyes."

He sighed, his shoulders slumping slightly, but he was still determined and angry. "Okay, yeah. I've seen it before. So what?"

"That symbol was on a shirt that one of the villagers in a small Tular town saw right after some women disappeared."

She could see gears grinding in his head. "And you think that their disappearance meant that something bad happened to them," he stated. He paused, his body tensing. Ella didn't know how she knew his muscles had tensed. Nothing about his demeanor changed. There was just a...stillness about him now. "What if they were taken to a safe place where they were given medicine and asked to help stop the traffickers who had hurt them?" he offered.

She watched his eyes, seeing something there. Ella wasn't sure what, but she'd been trained not to trust wealthy, powerful men. "Is that what happened?" she asked, the doubt apparent in her tone.

Malcolm shook his head slightly. "I don't know. I'm just offering a possibility."

"Fine," she whispered, suddenly aware that he was close again. How did he keep doing that?

"Fine...what?"

Ella suspected that she was going to regret her next comment, but figured she had to know. Keep one's friends close, and one's enemies closer, she reminded herself. "Fine, you can help me. We'll figure this out together."

He smiled, but the light in his eyes warned her that he wasn't smiling about her agreement. "Good. So what's next?" he asked.

She wasn't going to tell him that she was going to do some internet searching. It was pretty amazing what one could find just by surfing through some of the "back-door" chat sites. It's where she found most of her leads. "The first thing to do is to find out who is talking about things. Why don't you talk to your sources and ask around? See if anyone recognizes the flaming hand symbol."

"Fine. I'll get right on that," he said, his voice heavy and deep, obviously not impressed with her assignment. "And what are you going to do?"

"Same thing," she told him, although she didn't mention that she'd be doing it differently. But she was starting to think that he really didn't know anything about the trafficking. Or maybe there wasn't any trafficking going on. Okay, that wasn't true. Human trafficking happened on a daily basis, although most people were unaware of it.

"I'll let you know what I find out."

"Fine," he moved closer. "But one more thing," he began.

"What's that?" she asked. Unfortunately, she didn't move fast enough. Not mentally, or physically. Before she understood what he was going to do, Malcolm reached out and pulled her into his arms. Just like this afternoon, as soon as his lips touched hers, everything exploded. There was no hesitation this time either. As soon as he kissed her, Ella wrapped her arms around his neck, her fingers curling into his dark hair. It wasn't soft. She doubted anything about this man would be soft. But the whole kiss, everything about him was rough and heavy and powerfully enticing. His teeth nipped at her lips, demanding entry. When she opened her mouth, his tongue moved in, mating with hers, mocking her attempts to pull back until she was just as active a participant as he was.

For a long time, he kissed her and she clung to him, her body aching as she kissed him back. Ella wasn't sure who pulled back this time, but she would wager money that it hadn't been her. When he lowered his hands to his sides, she looked up at him, confused and wishing he'd continue. To pull her back into his arms and make love to her on the table behind her.

Then reality sunk into her lust-muddled mind and she remembered that she wasn't the type of woman to make love on a conference room table.

Stepping away from Malcolm was difficult, almost painful, but she managed it. She looked around, trying to locate her messenger bag. It was on the floor and she had no idea how it had gotten there. Hadn't it been on her shoulder before? No, she'd whipped it off, over her head and dumped it onto the conference room table so the contents would be handy, in case she needed a weapon of some kind.

Grabbing it now, she pulled it back over her head, settling the leather bag against her body as if it might protect her.

Goodness, if she had needed some form of defense, Ella doubted that she could have done anything about it. Apparently, Malcolm Reynolds, Marquis of Theeds, billionaire many times over, and her number one nemesis for the past several years, just had to kiss her and her mind turned to mush. Not good!

Turning, Ella walked out of his office for the second time that day.

And just as before, her knees were more than a little wobbly as she entered the elevator.

Chapter 5

Ella wandered through the aisles of clothing, not really seeing anything. Her mind wasn't on shopping, it was on Malcolm. More specifically, two nights ago when she'd lost herself in his arms, kissing him back as if there was no tomorrow.

What did that mean? Why had she so completely lost it with him? She never lost herself when she had sex. Okay, so she wasn't a particularly sexually active person. In her profession, finding someone to have sex with wasn't that high on her list of priorities. Staying alive had ranked much higher. She'd gone through wars and famines, reported on heinous crimes and had to dodge kidnappers on several occasions. Besides, one usually needed a bed for sex. Over the past few years, more often than not, she'd slept on the ground, in a hammock, in tents and, on really special occasions, on an air mattress. The few times she'd come home, Ella had stayed at her dad's house or in her tiny apartment. Again, not places that would make a woman feel especially sexy.

But still...her reactions to Malcolm were...overwhelming. Especially since she was trying to prove he was a criminal on a global scale. This story was huge, she could feel it in her bones. And despite her belief three days ago that Malcolm was at the center of this "flaming palm" mystery, something told her that Malcolm wasn't involved in sex trafficking. But...he'd recognized the symbol. She knew it! So, why had he lied to her? Why hadn't he just told her what he knew of the flaming palm?

Or was her intuition about him wrong, twisted by lust that seemed to flare up every time they were alone together? It didn't seem to matter where they were...an elevator, a warehouse, in his office...as soon as they were alone, the lust flared up, ready to consume them.

Ella didn't flatter herself that she would have stopped him last night. She'd been completely into the kiss, eager to take it further. Malcolm had been the one to pull away and she hated that. It gave him all the power and Ella preferred having the power in her own hands.

Still...maybe he wasn't the horrible person she'd thought he was all these years.

And yet, she still remembered her mother's tears the day she'd come home early from work at the estate. Malcolm's father had fired her, without any notice or severance pay, simply because she'd started losing her hair due to the chemo treatments. He'd said she was slacking off, but Ella knew her mother. She never slacked off. If anything, Ella's mother would have worked even harder, despite the ravages caused by the chemotherapy.

Ella moved along the racks of clothing, wondering why retail stores used circular racks instead of long, straight ones. Circular racks took up more space. They didn't seem to be more organized. And they forced a customer to shift in weird ways. Nope, circular racks were silly.

She picked up a pretty, lace bra, holding it up to the light. And why did women wear these things? Lace wasn't practical. Personally, she wore sports bras and cotton panties, preferring the comfort. Lace and satin...not practical when running down dirt pathways and dodging bullets.

Of course, Ella admitted she wasn't dodging bullets just now. So, maybe she *could* wear lace and satin when she was home? Ella put the pink bra back on the rack and picked up a black one. Would Malcolm like this on her? The lace was interesting and probably would show her nipples. She didn't know from personal experience, but she'd heard and read that men liked nipples. Her college boyfriend hadn't really been a breast man. He'd been more of a..., well, Ella suspected that Jimmy had been more of a man's man. She'd suspected that he was more into men than women. They'd broken up in college and remained friends. She called him whenever she traveled north to Scotland and he'd meet her in the capital for dinner or just drinks, whatever they had time for on that day.

"The black one would look amazing on you," a deep voice came from behind her.

Ella was so startled to see Malcolm that she dropped the bra. He chuckled knowingly as he picked it up. But when he stood, his tall body straightened slowly, as if he were contemplating every aspect of her figure, picturing her in the black lace. "Yes," he nodded, returning the lacy piece to her. "Definitely the black." Their eyes locked and her breath caught in her lungs. Instantly, she pictured herself in the black lace. In that picture, he was watching her as she slowly released the buttons of the blouse she was wearing. One by one. His eyes gazing at her fingers, waiting for every inch of skin revealed by her slow strip tease.

"Yes," he whispered hungrily.

"Do *not* kiss me here," she whispered forcefully. She didn't know what his favorite color was, or his favorite food. She knew what kind of car he drove, but not if he was a fast or cautious driver.

But Ella knew that look in his eyes. She'd seen it several times already and her heart accelerated, her stomach tightened. Anticipation, she thought. This was what it felt like.

"Where would you want me to kiss you?" he asked.

His words were so enticing, her tongue darted out, wetting her lips in anticipation of his kiss. She wanted that kiss! She wanted it more than she wanted to inhale again.

He lifted his hand, trailing a finger down her neck to her collar bone. "Here?" he asked softly. Had he just moved closer? Ella wasn't sure, too focused on that finger tracing a line along her skin. He actually pushed the material of her denim shirt out of the way, giving his finger more room. "Or maybe here?"

Ella realized that she was holding her breath. It was only the painful burn in her lungs that gave her the strength to inhale. Thankfully, the breath called to mind so many other things and she stepped back, shaking her head. "You're going to get us arrested," she muttered, looking away and putting the black lace bra back on the circular rack. She moved to the next rack, not wanting him to know that she'd been looking at bras. Which was absolutely stupid since he'd literally caught her looking at them, lifting them up to the light. Her only solace was that he didn't know what she'd been thinking in terms of the sheerness of the bra.

"Here," he said, handing her the black, lace bra that she'd just rejected. "I'll be able to see your nipples through this one." He pushed several more pieces out of the way. "I might not even need to take it off. I imagine that I'd be able to taste you through the material."

There was an odd sound after his comment and Ella was terrified that she'd just groaned. Images of him teasing her nipples through the sheer material of the bra caused her fingers to clench around the hanger. "We can't do this here," she whispered, needing to get away from him before she jumped him in the middle of the stupid circular racks. Crazily, her next thought was that, if they'd been straight, they might have hidden her ravenous attack more thoroughly.

"You're a C cup, right?' he asked. He was sorting through the bras and panties with an expertise that should have horrified her, but actually, it intrigued her. How experienced was he in selecting ladies lingerie? And why did his perceived expertise give her a stab of jealousy? It was silly to be jealous of his past lovers. Especially since she was still trying not to become one of his future lovers. Although, she wasn't doing a particularly good job of that. The past two times she'd been in his arms, her only consolation had been thinking of him being led away in handcuffs as her salvation from falling into his bed.

And even that image had been painful. Ella really wasn't thinking properly. She needed to force her thoughts back into this investigation and get it done before she made a colossal mistake.

He walked over to her and she might have laughed when he held a pair of pretty lace panties up against her butt. "What are you doing?" she hissed, shifting away from him.

"You're a size ten?" he asked, tilting his head from one side to the other, assessing her bottom.

"Yes!" she said, and turned away so that he couldn't see her butt. "Sometimes!" Her weight shifted a lot, depending on what she was doing. She could go down a size when she was out in the field, but when she came home, she devoured convenient, unhealthy foods and went up a size. That didn't mean she wanted him to know that though.

"You've got a great figure, Ella. Why hide it?"

"I don't hide it," she snapped, moving so that one of the racks hid her derriere. "There's a difference between hiding it from the world and hiding one's butt from a guy trying to size her up for lingerie purposes."

He didn't respond, but instead, moved back to the original rack and started matching up panties to the bras he'd already selected.

"What are you doing?" she demanded, glancing at the salesperson who was standing uncertainly off to the side, not sure if she should approach.

"I'm picking out bras and panties for you. Not the type of stuff you are probably wearing right now, but things that are sexier. Pieces I'd like to see you in."

She shook her head again. "I can't afford all of this!" she hissed, glancing towards the salesperson again.

"I'm buying it all for you," he told her, not bothering to look up as he added more pieces to the embarrassingly large pile.

"I am *not* going to wear those for you, Malcolm!" she told him firmly.

"Ella, there is something burning between us and we need to do something about it. Otherwise, whatever building we are in is going to catch fire. Now I think we should simply take care of this lust and get it out of the way. It's hot enough that it will eventually burn out. Then we can get back to our lives." He paused, looking almost angry with her for the situation they found themselves in. "Are you on board or are you going to keep trying to pretend this isn't happening?"

Ella opened her mouth, then closed it. What he said made sense. What she couldn't reconcile about the whole scenario was her mother and this hatred she'd had for Malcolm and his father for the past several years. Her mother had been so....desperate the afternoon she'd been fired. So humiliated! Not that she'd loved her job, but it had brought in an income and she was proud of the work she'd done for the estate. She'd cooked marvelous meals, cleaned up after the older man who was generally not very nice. Then to be summarily fired...and sick...well, Ella's mother hadn't been able to figure out how to move forward.

Maybe he was right. Perhaps she should use him just like his father used her mother all of those years ago. Could she do it? Could she use a man sexually and just walk away when their attraction burned out?

What was the alternative though? To continue to pretend as if there wasn't a crazy lust that consumed her every time they were within eyeshot of each other? That didn't make sense either.

And yet, Ella wasn't the kind of person who could use another. It was the whole point of her career. Ella loved exposing unfair circumstances so that public pressure, or law enforcement, forced the perpetrators to face their crimes. It was what she did, who she was.

"You're over analyzing this, Ella. It's just basic human nature."

She stared up at him, trying to reconcile everything. Unfortunately, there were too many issues coming at her. She couldn't keep up. "Is it though?" she asked him. "Are we really that animalistic that we should simply follow our urges?"

He smiled slightly at that. "Is that what you think is going on between us? Simple animalistic urges?" he mocked. Moving closer, he shook his head. "No, Ella. That's not what is happening. I agree that there is something primal about our need for each other. And yes, I feel a strong urge to pull you into that dressing room and do some pretty raunchy things to your delectable body." He paused, pulling her closer. "But that's not all that's happening, is it?"

Ella looked up into his eyes and silently acknowledged that her opinion of him had changed. From the night he'd saved her in the warehouse, she'd struggled to keep thinking of him as the bad guy. But if he wasn't the bad guy, then who was? And what was happening between them? Even now, as he pulled her closer to him, she wondered what he wanted from her. More importantly, she wondered if she could give that to him.

"You're moving too fast, Malcolm," she whispered. "I need time."

"How much time?" he asked as his fingers tightened on her waist.

She had to laugh at his impatience, although it also felt really nice. No man had ever wanted her like this. Yes, she'd had men find her attractive. But that was different.

"I don't know. Can we just...?"

"Yes. We can slow down," he said, finishing her sentence. He laughed slightly. "At least, we can try. Is that better? Does that give you the reassurance that you need?"

She smiled and, for the first time since she'd met him again, Ella moved closer to him. "Yes. Thank you."

He stared at her for a long moment, then sighed heavily and looked around. "You chose a damn good place for this conversation," he grumbled.

At the same moment, Ella looked around. It was at that moment that they both remembered where they were. "Good grief!" she laughed and stepped out of his arms.

"Exactly," he replied and pulled his wallet out of his pocket. "We need to talk," he ordered and picked up the bras and panties he'd selected. "I'll be right back."

"You're not buying those for me, are you?' she asked, horrified at the large stack of items. "Those bras are each about a hundred euros or more!"

He grinned, winking at her. "I can't wait to see you in each and every one of them." He walked away, handing the pieces to the salesperson. A few moments later, he returned and kissed her. It was just a brief caress but it felt shockingly nice.

"What was that for?" she asked.

"I wanted to kiss you. You looked kissable. So, I kissed you." He took her hand. "Come along," he urged. "We have things to do. I have a list."

She followed him, tugging at his arm to slow him down. "What kind of list?" she asked, looking around at the other shoppers self-consciously. Several women glanced in Malcolm's direction and Ella glared at them, furious that they would dare to flirt with him while he was walking next to her, holding her hand. How rude!

"A list of men who might be involved in that secret club you are so interested in."

She shot a stink eye to yet another woman, ignoring Malcolm's chuckle at her efforts. "You mean the secret club that you are also a member of?"

"If you say so," he replied and towed her into a store with beautiful, designer dresses. "I think you should try on this one," he suggested, handing her a red, sparkly dress with a deep V neckline.

Ella scoffed and ignored the dress. "I'd never wear something like that."

"Why not? You'd look amazing in it," he told her, but placed the dress back on the hook.

"Because those sparkles are nice and exciting, but every time my arm brushed against my side, the skin on the inside of my arm would get scraped. Not a comfortable dress."

He looked at the dress, then tilted his head as if conceding her point. "Okay, so pick out another dress."

"I don't need an evening gown, Malcolm. My world doesn't involve a lot of fancy parties."

"You're attending one with me tonight," he said and pointed to a gown of shimmering blue silk. "What about this one?"

Ella fingered the gown for a moment, then saw the price tag and gasped, pulling her hand away. "Not even on a dare!' she told him, moving towards the door of the store.

"I'll pay for the dress, Ella. But I need you at the event tonight."

She stopped and turned back to him, shifting her beat-up messenger back on her shoulder. "What kind of event? And why do you need me?"

He picked up another dress, one in maroon with a pretty, jeweled neckline. This one came up to her neck, but had a slit on the skirt that would probably show off most of her thigh when she moved.

"Because three of the men on our list will be attending. Since it's black tie, you need to dress up."

That captured her attention. "What list?"

"That list that I just mentioned. About the members of the secret club?"

She bit her lip, wanting to point out again that he was a member of the club. But shouldn't she simply prove it instead of stating it again?

"Fine. What time?" she asked.

He handed her three dresses and tilted his head towards the dressing rooms. "Go try these on."

"You can't buy me dresses," she protested.

He laughed. "Think of it as my punishment for whatever crimes I've committed in the past. You can wear one of the dresses tonight and then sell it at a consignment shop tomorrow, get several thousand dollars for it and give the money to charity. Doesn't that sound wonderful?"

She couldn't stop the chuckle at his suggestion. "Fine! I'll try on the dresses." She disappeared into the fitting room and tried on the first dress. She took off her jeans and tee-shirt, feeling painfully bourgeois to be shopping in a store like this one. But it felt pretty good too. She'd never really played dress up as a kid, preferring to run around outside in jeans, getting mud and grass stains on the knees. Only a couple of months ago, she'd been in a village surrounded by huge trees with wide, strong branches. In the afternoons, she'd climb into the trees and work on her story, writing what she'd discovered over the past twenty-four hours, or just sit in the tree reading quietly, the long branches allowing her to curl up and relax.

But as the shimmering fabric slipped over her figure, Ella couldn't suppress a small sigh of joy. The fabric was soft against her skin and, as she turned to look at herself in the mirror, she was stunned at the difference.

"Ella? Are you okay?" Malcolm called from the other side of the dressing room door.

Her fingers trembled as she touched the material, smoothing it over her figure slightly. "I'm fine!" she called back, but even to her own ears, her voice sounded strangled.

"What's wrong? Come out and let me see!"

Come out? Let him see? No way! She couldn't let him see her like this!

"Ella, come on out. Please?"

His voice was deep and commanding, but Ella continued to stare at herself in the mirror. Never in her wildest dreams would she have thought that she could look like this. The design of the dress made her waist look tiny, and the neckline draped over her chest, causing her average-sized breasts to look...bigger? No, that wasn't really the word. More enticing? Yes.

She looked like a pinup model from the fifties. Yes, that's what this dress did for her. She looked...sexy!

The dressing room door opened and Ella spun around. For a long moment, he didn't say anything. He simply stood there, taking in her figure in the shimmering dress. Then his eyes moved higher, looking directly into hers and he nodded. "Yes. That one will work nicely tonight." A moment later, he stepped out of the dressing room. "Try on the next one."

For a moment, she stood in the dressing room, stunned by her overwhelming reaction to the sensation of his eyes caressing her body. But then she snapped out of her trance-like state and reminded herself that she didn't even like the man. "I thought this one would work," she called back to him.

"It's perfect. But we might need other dresses. I don't know what we'll discover tonight, so it's better to have options for the future."

Ella let her fingers slide down the material of the next dress, almost afraid to try it on. And yet, eager at the same time! How could she have so many conflicting emotions running through her head?

Ella was a practical kind of person. When she needed food, she ate.

If she needed clothing, she pulled on a pair of jeans. Prior to meeting Malcolm, her life had been fairly black and white. Now she was surfing through shades of grey, and she wasn't sure how to surf!

"Here's another one," she heard his deep voice as he opened the door and...stopped. "You haven't changed." He handed her a strapless black dress done in silk. "Try this one next," he ordered and stepped out of the dressing room. "Come out here when it's on."

She huffed a bit as she stood there in the dressing room. "You're getting a bit dictatorial, Malcolm." But she still pulled off the first dress and slid into the black silk. There was no way she'd admit to him that she was just as eager to try on the dress as he was to see her in it. That would give him too much power. Balance, she thought as she slid the zipper up here back. Unfortunately, she couldn't get it all the way up and the bodice gaped in front of her as she twisted and contorted, trying to pull up the zipper.

"You okay?"

"I'm fine!" she called back to him. But he must have heard the frustration in her voice because a moment later, he stepped into the dressing room.

"I'll get that," he told her. His voice was huskier. Deeper. And as he moved behind her, she saw his eyes in the mirror. They were a dark, intense blue, conveying that his lust just under the surface was barely controlled.

"I don't need your help," she whispered, afraid of him touching her. It had been one thing when she'd had clothes on. But in this dress, her back and shoulders were bare. Skin to skin. He'd touch her! He would...

She gasped when his fingers slid along her spine. He watched her shiver under his fingers. When his fingers caressed her skin, it only confirmed what was in his mind. "You're not zipping up the dress," she whispered to him, their eyes staring at each other as their heartbeats pounded.

"I'm not?"

She shook her head.

"Maybe, I think it looks perfect just like this," he teased.

She rolled her eyes and shifted the material so it more completely covered her breasts. "Do you really want me at an event looking like this? With the dress half-zipped?"

He laughed and zipped up the dress. "I suspect that, if we were alone, we would be very late for whatever gathering was on the agenda."

Ella suspected that he was right. And unfortunately for her peace of mind, she wasn't sure if it would only be him doing the delaying. The way he'd touched her sent shivers of awareness shooting through her. Delicious shivers. Amazing shivers. Ella wasn't even sure that she cared about being in a dressing room.

He stood behind her, looking at her figure draped in black silk. His hands slid up her arms to rest on her bare shoulders as his eyes continued to sizzle. "We'll take this one as well."

Ella sighed. The dress cost several thousand dollars! "I can't buy these," she told him. "My bank balance is pretty good right now, but these dresses are way out of my price range."

"You're not buying them," he repeated. "Remember, the cost of these dresses is the first part of my punishment for my misdeeds," he told her, then slid the zipper back down. All the way down. The end of the zipper allowed her underwear to peek out and he looked down, noticing. One long finger even slid over the elastic of her panties. She couldn't see his eyes, but she was fairly sure that she knew what he was thinking. Mostly because she was thinking the same thing.

"Malcolm!" she whispered, clutching the dress to her breasts, but she couldn't finish her sentence.

He looked up, watching her in the mirror. "The next time you wear this dress, I'm going to make love to you just like this," he told her. Then he bent his head, gently kissing down her neck and along her bare shoulder. A moment later, he stepped out of the dressing room.

It took Ella several minutes before she could move. And when she did, it was to lean a hand against the mirror. Taking in deep gulps of air, she tried to slow her pounding heart rate. The kisses hadn't been overtly sexual, but there'd been the promise of pleasure in his touch, in his kiss. It was shattering!

"Ma'am?" a female voice called. "Your husband asked me to see if you need assistance."

Ella blinked at the still closed door, willing her body to stop trembling. She couldn't go out there like this. Her knees barely supported her, her hand braced against the mirror. "I'm fine!" she lied, closing her eyes to banish the image of Malcolm kissing her from her mind.

He was cheating, she thought and pushed away from the mirror. Straightening, she shucked the dress off and...hesitated. She wanted to toss it into the corner, crumpled in a ball. But it was a stunning dress and she loved the designer too much to disrespect the dress like that. Instead, she carefully hung the dress back on the hangar and pulled on her own clothes. There were still two other dresses that Malcolm had suggested she try on, but Ella determined that trying on anything else was a bad idea at this point. Jeans and her tee-shirt were a safer choice.

Stepping out of the dressing room, she left all of the dresses hanging there, determined not to allow Malcolm to buy any of them. "Thank you for your help," she said to the salesperson.

"Not a problem, ma'am," she replied with a smile, then stepped around her to collect the dresses. "I'll just get these wrapped up for you." And she took all four of the dresses.

"Oh, I'm not buying any of them," Ella told her firmly.

The woman smiled, tilting her head as if she thought Ella was being cute. "Your husband has already paid for all four of them, ma'am."

Ella gritted her teeth, not sure if she liked being called "ma'am", but very certain that she didn't like Malcolm going behind her back and buying her dresses that were...well, she could buy a brand new car for the same amount of money!

"Malcolm, you're not buying me anything," she told him as soon as she stepped out of the dressing room area.

"I'm not?" he asked, looking up from his cell phone. He was leaning a shoulder against the wall, obviously waiting for her.

"No! Those dresses are too expensive and...!" Before she could finish her comment, the salesperson stepped up with the dresses already encased in a protective, plastic wardrobe bag.

"It was a pleasure, my lord," she said, smiling up at Malcolm.

Ella sighed, then turned to glare up at him. "Why are you helping me? As soon as I figure this out, you're going to prison."

He laughed softly and put a hand to the small of her back, ignoring the horrified look on the salesperson's face as he led her out of the store. "Maybe I'm daring you to figure this out," he told her.

She thought about that for a moment, and nodded. "Okay, I can see that. You're arrogant enough to think I'm not smart enough. Or your secret-club cronies are powerful enough that anything I discover will be suppressed. Do they all have a 'get out of jail free' card?" she asked, suspiciously.

He chuckled as they left the boutique. "I suspect that some of them do. But I have every confidence that you will be able to not only get enough evidence to stop their efforts to avoid prosecution, but that your writing is powerful enough to convince public sentiment that something has to change in the system." He looked down at her as he opened the back of his car. "You've demonstrated the power of your writing before. Don't let me down."

Chapter 6

Ella smoothed the burgundy evening gown over her hips, twisting from right to left in an effort to see how she looked. The bodice was covered in sparkling jewels and reached her neck. It was sleeveless, and hugged her breasts and tapered at her waist. Thankfully, the skirt was several dozen layers of burgundy chiffon. No thigh slits and nothing see through.

She hadn't accepted the garment bag from Malcolm after trying on all of the dresses. But as soon as she'd pulled into the parking lot of her tiny apartment, a delivery person with the dresses and the bag of lingerie was waiting for her. She didn't even have to sign for the delivery. The man just smiled professionally and handed both bags to her as soon as she'd stepped out of her car. The dratted man hadn't given her a chance to refuse the delivery. He was gone before she'd even closed her car door.

So, now she was the proud owner of four evening gowns and a lot of sexy, expensive lingerie.

She'd also received a text message from his assistant with the time that Malcolm would pick her up and the names of the people they were trying to connect with. Ella had stared at the text message, recognizing several of the names. They'd come up in her research, plus she knew that those men had traveled to several of the countries where "flaming hand" sightings had occurred.

Those names were the only reason she was dressed and ready to attend this event tonight. At least, that's what she told herself. Ella stared at her reflection in the mirror, realizing that there was a betraying level of excitement emanating from her. Was that because she was going to find out more information on her investigation? Or was it because she was about to see Malcolm again?

Ella tried very hard to be honest with herself. And deep down inside, she knew that her excitement was due to the anticipation of seeing Malcolm tonight.

She also suspected that he wasn't the man she'd originally thought him to be. He was helping her to investigate what was going on with this "flaming hand" thing. He was going out of his way to provide information as well as access to places that would normally be out of her reach.

After spending time with him for the past several days, Ella had to admit that he wasn't acting like a man trying to hide something. Her gut told her that he was innocent. Even more, it seemed as if he wanted to discover the truth as well. But her instincts also told her that he knew more than he let on.

"I can do this," she told her reflection. And with a nod of confidence, she turned away from the mirror, enjoying the way the chiffon skirt fluttered around her legs. She'd even pinned her hair up and added a pair of faux diamond earrings. She looked and felt sexy.

"Time to get more leads," she muttered as she grabbed her evening bag. Ella wasn't foolish enough to let Malcolm pick her up at her apartment door. After their last few interludes, she understood the risk that they wouldn't manage to leave her apartment. Instead, she walked to the lobby of her apartment building, stepping out of the elevator just as a long, elegant limousine pulled up outside of the door.

For a fraction of a second, Malcolm looked surprised as she stepped out of the building just as he was getting out of the limousine, but quickly, his gaze took in her figure in the burgundy dress and his surprise was replaced by admiration. "You look lovely." he told her as he took her hand.

Ella smiled up at him. "Thank you for the dress."

He lifted her hand to his lips and kissed her fingertips. "It is my pleasure," he told her, his voice deep and sexy.

She slipped into the dark interior and took a deep, calming breath. When Malcolm stepped in after her, she scooted over, but he took her hand, stopping her from moving away. "Just enjoy tonight, Ella. Nothing is going to happen that you don't want to happen."

That was part of the problem, she thought. Honesty wasn't always a comfortable thing, but she had to admit that she wanted him. And even more, she trusted him. She wasn't sure exactly when that had happened. She'd come back from her last assignment, determined to put this man in prison. Nor was she sure why she trusted him, but her instincts insisted that he wasn't the bad guy. History and the way his father had treated her mother had influenced her opinion of him. But

Ella knew that father and son were different people.

"You don't live on the estate with your father?" she asked.

"No," he replied, looking straight ahead.

"Why not?"

Ella held her breath, suspecting that his answer would be very important. Both what he said and what he didn't say.

"My father and I don't agree on a lot of issues."

"He doesn't want you living at the main house?" she probed, needing clarification.

Malcolm laughed, shaking his head as he lifted her hand to his lips again. "My father repeatedly demands that I move back to the house and live on the estate," he replied, but didn't add that there wasn't a chance in hell that it would ever happen. No, his issues with Edward were private. As much as he wanted to spend several days and nights with Ella wrapped around his body as he made love to her in every conceivable way, the bottom line was that Ella was a reporter. He'd never aired his dirty laundry in the past and he wasn't going to start now.

His father was a monster. Looking out the window, he wondered if his father would ever receive the punishment that he deserved. Ella's investigation into the flaming hand pin was a start. But what did it all mean? Malcolm knew that his father was a member of that society. The news that someone had seen the flaming heart symbols in a small village on another continent bothered him deeply. He and his friends had started the group as a counter to the ridiculous flaming palm society. Members of that group truly were human traffickers, stealing young people, both boys and girls, out of vulnerable villages and selling them on the black market. He knew that Jenna had caught wind of someone trying to steal girls out of Tular lately, but he'd thought that their group had put a stop to it.

Had someone within the new group decided to advertise their efforts? Some members had brought up the issue of publicity before. And that would make sense with the sightings Ella mentioned. There had been four women who had been near death in a small village in Tular. And yes, he and Jenna had arranged for those girls to be picked up and delivered to a hospital in Germany. But he and Jenna, and most of the other members of their group, had decided to keep their activities quiet in order to maintain their ability to move in and out of countries more easily. It allowed better efficiency of their efforts. So, had someone decided to go rogue?

It was possible. The more people who joined their organization, the more opinions were involved.

He looked down and realized that Ella was still waiting for an answer. "My father and I aren't close."

"So...living together isn't a possibility?"

"Not a possibility." He decided that a change in subject would be a good idea before she probed the issue of his relationship with his father too deeply. There were things in his past that were better left in the past. Probing would resolve nothing.

"The men you'll meet tonight might be a bit..." he searched for the right word. "Chauvinistic," he informed her. "And we might get more information from them if you play along with their...beliefs."

Ella looked confused for a moment, then she smiled as if the idea were intriguing. Damn, she was amazing!

"I remember hearing one of the teachers at my high school boarding school tell another teacher that, if they remained silent during field trips, the students in the van or bus would forget that an authority figure was around. The teacher explained that she learned most of what was going between the students during those road trips." She laughed. "So I'm supposed to play dumb and silent tonight, is that the strategy?"

He chuckled, looking at her strangely. "This might be a bad idea."

"Why's that?" she laughed, and he wondered if Ella was aware of her fingers tangling with his.

"You might be a bit too smart to play dumb."

She laughed outright. "I don't think anyone has ever complimented me so beautifully!" and she leaned her head against his shoulder for a brief moment. When she lifted her head up, Ella looked startled, as if she hadn't meant to be openly affectionate.

Malcolm chuckled at her expression. "Don't worry, Ella. I won't assume anything. Let's just have fun tonight, okay?" He leaned back in the leather seat. "You play dumb and I'll ask leading questions." He squeezed her hand. "If you want to pretend a bit of drunkenness, that might go a long way towards convincing these men that you're invisible and harmless."

"Ah, what every woman aspires to be; invisible around strong, powerful men!"

The limousine pulled up outside of a massive house that looked as if it might be a castle, except that it was less than ten years old. There was something about older houses that seemed to exude dignity and reverence. But this house gave the impression that it continued to yell "Look at me!" instead. Such a sad state of affairs. In a country filled with beautiful, old houses, the owner of this one had to fake it with a pretend-old house.

The driver pulled up to the curb and someone immediately opened the back door. Malcolm exited first and turned to offer his hand to Ella.

"Good evening, Lord Theeds," the butler greeted him.

As they walked into the house, Ella took Malcolm's hand, her eyes wide as she feigned excitement at the pretentiousness. "Do you think we'll see any movie stars?" Ella asked, adding a note of breathlessness to her voice.

Malcolm laughed and patted her hand. "Anything is possible, my dear. Let me get you something to drink."

"Oh, goody!" she replied, playing her part perfectly.

Malcolm chuckled and, to further convince anyone who might be watching, she pressed herself against his arm and looked around. Ella pretended to be awed by the enormous foyer with the shimmering chandelier, but in reality, she was stunned by the muscles underneath Malcolm's tuxedo jacket. For a member of the aristocracy, she hadn't thought that he would be buff. Handsome, yes. But not strong and muscular. Weren't aristocrats supposed to be lazy and indolent?

They stepped out onto a large balcony and a man with a booming voice called out, "Marquis of Theeds," to the crowd below. There was a slight pause in the volume of the conversation in the area and most of the room turned and look up. Malcolm ignored it, feigning indifference. He really didn't give a damn about any of this. Most of the men in this room were over the age of sixty. Meanwhile, the women hanging on the arms of the gentlemen were in their early to mid-twenties. The ladies all wore glittering dresses that revealed almost as much skin as they covered. Obviously, these women weren't chosen to be companions for their business intellect.

Then Malcolm looked down at Ella, thinking of her last article, which had outlined the corruption in that mid-east government. That piece had resulted in the arrest of several government officials, including two royal princes.

Never underestimate a woman, he told himself. Ella was playing the part of the beautiful ditz perfectly, looking around with wide, amazed eyes. But she was one of the smartest people he knew. He wondered why Ella didn't write a book about her experiences. Why did she prefer to dive into the worst, most dangerous situations in the world, find an injustice, and then tell the world about it?

Because she wasn't *just* brilliant, he thought as he looked around, taking in the pompous, overbearing, overweight men that moved forward to greet him. Ella was brave and had a huge, giving heart. Which only made him want to help her more.

"Theeds!" someone called out, using his title instead of his name. He hated that. As Marquis of Theeds, he wished the title would just fall off the face of the earth. But his father, the Duke of Theeds, loved the importance that everyone conveyed upon him because of his title. As a duke, Edward Reynolds ranked higher than almost every man in this room. "It's great that you finally attended one of our exclusive soirees! It's about time!"

Malcolm turned and greeted the man. "Ella, this is Lord Heron, Count of Masser," he said, introducing Ella to the rotund man. "Lord Heron, it is my pleasure to introduce you to Ella, my guest for the evening."

Ella beamed and curtsied. It took all of Malcolm's discipline not to laugh outright at her social gaffe. Especially since he knew that Ella was very aware that one didn't curtsy to a lord. Hell, she hadn't even curtsied to him!

"Goodness, I'm delighted to meet you, Lord Heron!" Ella gushed.

Heron chuckled and extended his hand. Unfortunately, it also happened to be the arm that his sparkly lady was hanging onto. She had to release his arm and pouted beautifully while she waited for Heron to release Ella's hand.

"And what do you do, my dear?"

Ella smiled and looked around. "Oh, well, I write," she replied honestly.

The aging earl chuckled with a patronizing tone. "What sorts of books do you write?"

Ella waved that away. "Oh, I haven't written a book yet. But maybe. In the future."

Malcolm looked at her curiously, especially since he'd been wondering that exact same thing. "Really? You'd write a book?"

Ella giggled and squeezed his arms. "Doesn't everyone want to write the next best-selling novel?"

The count laughed and nodded with a patronizing smile. "Everyone tries! And you should never give up your hopes and dreams, my dear."

"Really?" she asked earnestly. Malcolm watched her and wanted to laugh, but she was doing such an excellent job, he couldn't ruin her efforts.

They chatted with the count and his girlfriend for several more minutes, then moved on, greeting others. Ella was astonished by how many members of the British aristocracy were present tonight and amused at how many were eager to welcome Malcolm into their ranks. There were several interesting interactions when someone asked Malcolm if his father was planning to attend the night's activities. At every inquiry, Malcolm easily deflected the question, neither answering or ignoring it. She was amazed at how he controlled the conversation.

But what was even more disturbing, besides all of these married men laughing and drinking with women other than their wives, was how bored she was. So many people worked their whole lives to be included into an event such as this one. The desire to talk and be included among the highest ranks of society was what some people lived and breathed to accomplish.

Growing up, Ella had wondered what the big, fancy parties were like at Malcolm's estate. She'd been jealous of what may or may not have happened during the big social gatherings and imagined stories about what she thought was happening. Of course, in her imagination, she was the veteran reporter who covered all of the events.

Now, standing among all of these people, she had to stifle a yawn. Much to her chagrin, this kind of a gathering wasn't the amazing, glittering event that she'd pictured all those years ago. In reality, it was... boring. Tedious! There weren't any interesting conversations happening, no good-natured political debates or intense financial revelations, no shocking business deals being made. It was just a bunch of pretentious, self-righteous, overweight men drinking heavily and pretending to be important because they had a beautiful woman on their arm.

"I'll be right back," she whispered, trying not to interrupt the conversation about a man's fishing expedition. He was bragging about catching the biggest fish that day, but he was so drunk he kept forgetting to say that he was the one that reeled in the big fish. Several times, he'd accidentally mentioned the ship's captain, who had stepped in to save the fish.

Malcolm held onto her hand for a moment, looking down at her. "You okay?" he asked softly, whispering in her ear.

Ella shivered, and hoped he didn't notice. "I'm fine," she replied. "Just need to find the ladies room."

He moved closer, lowering his voice as he said into her ear, "You're coming back, right? If I have to listen to one more golf or fishing story, I'm going to do something drastic. I can't be held accountable for my actions."

Ella laughed, then realized that she was slipping out of character and suppressed her amusement. "Behave!" she hissed back at him, then slipped away. She had no idea where the restrooms were, but she didn't care either. As long as she got away for a few moments where she could relax her cheek muscles and stop smiling at inane, tedious stories.

After several wrong turns, she found a bathroom and stepped in with a sigh of relief. Her feet were killing her and she wanted to get rid of this stupid dress. She would kill for a pair of sweatpants right about now!

Not literally, she corrected mentally as she walked to one of the mirrors. Her lipstick was still in place, but she pulled out a tube of lipstick anyway and touched up the edges. Two other women walked in, talking and appeared to be just as bored now that they were in front of their men.

"Can you believe that stupid story about climbing Mount Everest?" a woman in a pink, low cut dressed groaned. Her friend in a blue dress, shuddered.

"No! I don't believe any of the stories these blowhards tell at these stupid events. They are all lies."

Pink-Dress laughed. "Even if he did make it to the top of Mount Everest, I read an article that talked about how it's actually the Sherpas who do all of the real work. If it weren't for them, none of us silly Europeans would make it up the mountain."

"Yeah, well, it makes these guys think they are strong, powerful men. So, I don't care."

Blue Dress took her lipstick out and smiled to Ella. "Nice dress," she said. "Who are you with?"

Ella was stunned to be addressed. For so long tonight, she'd pretended to be invisible and, for the most part, it had worked. The men mingling with the other beautiful women rarely deigned to look in her direction. If they did, it was merely to ogle her breasts before comparing Ella to the woman on their arm. So it was startling that someone addressed her directly.

"Oh, um...I'm here with Malcolm Reynolds," she said, wondering if she should have said "Marquis" or something more formal.

No need, she realized moments later.

"The Marquis of Theeds?" Pink-Dress exclaimed.

Blue-Dress was equally impressed. "Goodness, I'd love to be with him! He's the only man in here who can actually see his feet!"

Both ladies laughed as they checked their perfect hair, shifting a pin or two as if that did something dramatic to their appearance. Ella suspected that they were just as bored with the party as she was and trying to find reasons to linger here in the bathroom rather than head back out and listen to the men who most likely paid their bills.

A cynical assumption, and they were probably making the same assumption about her. But hey, it's a mercenary world out there!

"He's a very nice man," Ella replied.

Blue Dress laughed. "Nice? He's hot and not fat! *And* he probably has ten times as much money as the rest of those idiots out there combined!"

Pink Dress groaned. "Damn, I bet he'd buy me that Fendi bag! You know, the blue one that would go with my blue shoes?"

"Seriously? There's no way any of these men would buy a Fendi bag! Those kinds of gifts are reserved for the wife-side of the equation," Blue Dress admonished, then dabbed at her lipstick. "Look at the time. We have maybe an hour before show time."

Ella blinked. "Show time? What's that?"

They both blinked at her with astonishment. "You're new to this whole mistress thing, right?" Pink Dress chuckled.

Blue Dress reached into her dress and lifted her breasts so they were more visible. "Show Time is when we perform."

"Perform?" Ella echoed, still not sure what they meant. There was no way she was getting up on stage!

"Perform?" Pink Dress repeated, as if the answer were obvious. "On our men? The whole reason they take us out?"

Blue Dress laughed. "My guy promised that he would take me to Tular for his next business trip. For that, he gets a bit of special attention."

Pink Dress shrugged. "Don't fall for it," she warned. "I was there last month and it was a total drag! And I don't even know why he brought me. There were other women that he was more interested in. Besides, it was really hot and uncomfortable there. Not even the hotel had air conditioning could break through that heat."

Ella's ears perked up. Tular? Women? "What did you do while you were there?" she asked, pretending as if her heart wasn't racing with anticipation.

"I watched television," Blue Dress said with a shudder. "The shopping wasn't worth the trip and my guy left me in the hotel room while he went out and did something weird. I don't know what it was, but it sounded like hunting." She pulled back from the mirror and looked at her reflection, turning from side to side and pressing a hand to her stomach as if that movement could flatten it more than it was already. "For all I know, he went on one of those illegal safari hunting trips." She shrugged and turned towards the door. "You've been warned!" Blue Dress announced with a laugh. "Stay away from exotic-sounding adventures!"

"My guy told me he'd buy me some pretty jewelry."

Ella bit her lip, trying to keep herself from warning these two ladies that the gems mined in Tular weren't done with ethical staffing solutions. Some of the mines used child labor, which was slave labor. From the looks of them, Ella didn't think that they'd care as long as they received a shiny rock for their performance efforts.

Ella tucked her lipstick back into her evening bag as casually as possible. "Well, it sounds like anyplace in Africa would be pretty hot right about now. Isn't the equator somewhere around there?" she asked.

Pink Dress shrugged. "That's up near the north pole," she explained, putting a hand on Ella's shoulder. "It's easy to get those things mixed up with the penguin region."

Ella bit her tongue and nodded in agreement. She didn't explain that penguins actually lived in Antarctica, which was on the South Pole. And the equator wasn't anywhere near the North Pole. Instead, she followed the two women out of the bathroom. Puffins! Puffins could be found near the North Pole! They were pretty cute, but penguins generally stole all of the cold-weather attention.

Ella followed at a more sedate pace, not interested in returning too quickly. Pink and Blue had mentioned something about the party winding down and their required "performance" becoming imminent.

She didn't want to perform, but Ella couldn't deny that she'd been painfully aware of Malcolm all evening. She'd stood by his side, either hugging his arm, or with his arm around her waist, his heavy hand resting against her hip or the small of her back. Occasionally, his hand had slipped lower and she'd held her breath, waiting, wondering if he would do something outrageous.

He never did, but when he moved his hand higher, she would glance up at him and see his smirk.

In other words, she'd been on edge all night! Her mind might be bored, but her body wasn't. Her body was incredibly aware of Malcolm and his strength as well as the never-ending tension that seemed to vibrate between them.

Even now, she stepped into the room and looked for Malcolm. She located him over near the fireplace and it wasn't simply because he was the tallest man in the room. There was just something about him that drew her gaze.

He must've felt it as well because he looked towards her. Eyes clashing, he lifted his drink to his lips, not releasing her from that hold he had over her.

He dared her with that look. Ella couldn't resist him. As if in a trance, she moved towards him. The crowd might have parted or she might have simply shifted in between the mingling bodies. Ella wasn't sure, nor did she care. Malcolm was watching her as she came to him.

When she was only a few feet away, he extended his hand towards her. Without hesitation, Ella placed her hand in the warmth of his and...it felt right. Good! Exciting!

"Let's go," he growled into her ear.

Ella stared up into his eyes for a long moment, reading his intent. Did she want this? "Yes!" she replied, both to herself as well as to Malcolm's unspoken question.

Malcolm's fingers tightened on her waist. It was there in her eyes as well as in the way her body swayed towards him. She trusted him! Damn, that felt better than it should!

He squeezed her hand. Yet another pompous jerk sidled up to him, eager for conversation. But Malcolm wasn't in the mood to speak to anyone now. He didn't want to hear about a fishing story or a trip to the Bahamas, a great swing at one at the golf courses that was probably a lie anyway. He didn't want to reassure some idiot that their investments were in a good place or pretend that he might consider a business deal.

Malcolm wanted to be alone with Ella so that he could explore her amazing body. He knew her mind. Loved her mind. But tonight was all about the physical. He wanted to make love to her until this insane urgency subsided. He wanted to walk into a room, see her and be able to ignore the immediate pain of lust, the need to pull her into his arms and make her his.

She followed him willingly. Eagerly! They made their way through the thinning crowd. Several people called out to him, but Malcolm nodded to some and completely ignored others. No matter what they wanted to talk about, he wasn't interested.

It was a testament to the excellent service in this place that someone had realized he was leaving and had called his driver. The man was standing outside, holding the back door to the limousine open so that Ella and Malcolm could step inside.

As soon as the driver closed the door, Malcolm turned to Ella, needing to pull her into his arms and kiss her. But she was already moving towards him, sliding into his arms as if she were water, melting into him. His mouth covered hers and he kissed her, feeling her arms wrap around his neck as their tongues danced together. There was no preface to this kiss, no teasing nips or tastes. They were too hungry for each other and Malcolm loved that her eagerness almost matched his own need.

As the driver guided the limousine through the quiet streets of London, Malcolm learned more about Ella's body. About where she wanted to be touched. He was careful not to release any clasps or slide down any zippers. Not yet. But his hands found bare skin under the burgundy chiffon, sliding along her legs. He absorbed her gasps of pleasure into his mouth as he continued to explore her.

Thankfully, it didn't take long to arrive at Ella's apartment. The limousine came to a smooth stop right in front and he pulled her hands from him. "We're here. I'm coming inside, Ella. If you don't want this, tell me now."

She stared up at him and, for a startled moment, he thought she might say no. But then her kiss-swollen lips curled upwards and she nodded. "Yes. Definitely!"

He let out the breath he'd been holding, then nodded sharply as the driver opened the back door. "Let's go," he took her hand. Exiting first, he held her hand to help her out, ensuring that she didn't trip on the long dress. But once they were both standing on the sidewalk, he turned to his driver and said, "We're done for the night. I'll call you when I need you."

The man tipped his hat and closed the back door. "Very good, my lord." He walked to the front of the limousine.

Malcolm couldn't wait any longer. With her hand still in his, he led her into the building at a fast pace, wanting to be inside of her apartment so that he could strip off over her clothes and see her. Feel her. Touch every part of her and learn what made her scream.

Ella fumbled with the keys to her apartment. Gently, Malcolm took the keys from her trembling fingers and, pressing his chest against her back, reached around her to unlock the door. She sighed with relief when the door swung open, but Malcolm spun her around, pressing her against the wall just inside of the doorway. With his foot, he kicked the door closed while, at the same time, his hands pulled her back into his arms. "Love the dress," he said. "But it has to go. I want you naked!"

She whimpered and reached up to tug the knot on his bow tie. The ends pulled everything loose and she tossed the scrap of black material away. While she worked the buttons on his shirt, his fingers deftly found the hooks at the back of her neck. It was easier for him to reveal what was underneath her dress than it was for Ella to unbutton his shirt.

As the dress whispered to the floor, he stepped back, looking at her in nothing but a pair of lace panties and heels. "You aren't wearing a bra!" he growled, looking at her perfect breasts. They weren't large, but they were perfect! Round and pert with raspberry colored nipples that were hard and pointing towards him, obviously eager for his touch.

She stared up at him, but Malcolm couldn't pull his gaze away from her beautiful breasts. His hands moved from her waist, sliding higher and higher until they cupped her breasts, feeling their weight. They were perfect in his hands, soft and supple. Slowly, his thumb moved higher and higher, circling her nipple but not quite touching it. Malcolm savored the anticipation, savored her trembling with anticipation. Her eyes were closed now and Malcolm watched her back arch, her body silently begging him to touch her nipples.

When his thumbs finally slid over the tips, she gasped. Ella's hands had been pressed against the wall during the moments leading up to this, but when his thumbs teased her nipples, she grabbed his wrists. For a moment, he thought she might try to pull his hands away. It wouldn't work, he thought as the desire intensified. Instead, her hands held onto his wrists, guiding his hands, showing him what she wanted him to do. It was so hot, watching her guide his hands. He couldn't wait for her to show him what else she liked!

Ella couldn't take the torture any longer! She whimpered and started to pull his hands away, but he pinched her nipples, ever so slightly, and the desire was like a lightning bolt that shot straight from her nipples to her core. "Malcolm!" she groaned. Then her hands moved from his wrists, fighting the stupid buttons on his tuxedo shirt. If she had a pair of scissors, she would have simply cut the shirt off. In the end, her fingers couldn't work fast enough for either of them. Malcolm pushed the tuxedo jacket off his shoulders and tossed it onto the kitchen countertop, then went to work on the obnoxiously small buttons on his tuxedo.

Ella didn't wait for the shirt to come off. As soon as skin was revealed, her fingers moved against his chest, feeling the warmth of his skin, the roughness of his chest hair with a tempting line going from the center of his chest straight down...only to be lost behind his slacks.

"Take them off!" she demanded, fumbling with the button of his slacks.

"I'll do it," he growled right back, moving her hands away and putting them back on his chest. "Touch me, Ella!"

She did! And he made sexy, grunting noises as her hands slid over the broad expanse of his chest. He was amazing! Every part of him was rock hard, covered with muscles that ridged his arms, shoulders, and stomach. Malcolm was definitely no aristocrat slouch. He worked out hard and his efforts were...beautiful!

Ella could barely breathe as she watched him toss his slacks on top of his tuxedo jacket, then pushed his boxer briefs off as well. She had no idea when he'd discarded his shoes and socks, nor did she care. When he stood up, the man was gloriously naked.

"Bedroom!" he snapped, and picked her up.

Ella gasped when she felt his erection pressing against her core as she wrapped her arms around his neck. "There," she said, tilting her head towards the only door in the apartment.

He carried her through the door to her bedroom, carefully lowered her down onto the bed, and stretched out beside her. He only pulled back enough to slide her panties off, dropping them on the floor before moving back between her legs, tossing several condoms onto the comforter beside them. Ella was vaguely aware and relieved that he had remembered protection, although she kept a box of condoms in her bedside drawer. They'd been there for a long time, and she didn't have the brain capacity to wonder if they were expired by this point.

Especially with Malcolm looking at her like that. She was completely naked, wearing only a pair of black pumps. "These stay," he decided as he slid his hand from her ankle to her outer thigh, pressing her legs wider as he moved between her legs.

She thought he'd go for her breasts again. Ella wanted him to touch her breasts. Her nipples ached to feel him touch her with his mouth, his fingers...anything at all! But his mouth moved against her neck, discovering spots she hadn't realized existed. With each discovery, she writhed against him, feeling his erection against her stomach or thigh and wanting him inside her. Ella was so ready for him, she wanted to cry but she didn't know how to say so!

"Please!" she whimpered, almost sobbing with her need for him to ease the ache between her legs. Rubbing her thighs against his hips, she arched into him. Malcolm only moved lower, his mouth latching onto one aching nipple while his hand moved to tease the other breast, tweaking her nipple. His mouth was hot and shockingly good! Her fingers dove into his hair, holding his head in place while she cried out. He moved to the other nipple and teased it for long moments while Ella trembled and shifted against him, trying to find some relief.

"No more! I can't take any more!" she screamed, pulling his head away from her breast. She turned her head to the side, spotting the condom amid the rumpled comforter and tore it open.

"Give it to me, Ella," he ordered, reaching for it.

"No! I want to do it!" and she pressed against his shoulders until he pulled back, kneeling in front of her.

Ella stared at him, shocked at how large he was. This whole time, she'd only touched his shoulders and stomach. Then he'd picked her up and...!

"Ella!" he snapped. Impatiently, he took the condom and rolled the protection down over his erection. "You're too slow and I'm already too turned on."

She laughed, delighted that she could do to him what he'd been doing to her this whole time.

With another growl, he pressed her back against the mattress, covering her body with his own. "Oh, you think it's funny that I'm on the edge here?" he asked. His hand moved from her waist to her leg, sliding it up higher so that he was more perfectly cradled against her hips. "I think I'm going to have to punish you for your amusement at my expense."

Ella felt his erection press into her and gasped, gripping his shoulders as she lifted her hips. "Does my punishment include...?" She closed her eyes as he pressed into her, easing into her tight, wet folds. "Yes!" she sighed. Her frantic need was momentarily appeased as he pushed deeper and deeper into her body. Then he pulled out and she grabbed his arms, her eyes flashing open as the friction from his body teased her. "No!"

"Yes," he countered and thrust into her again. Dancing, their bodies came together and retreated, pressing into her and sliding away. With every thrust, their bodies arched towards each other, the tempest rising, their need growing out of control.

"Faster!" she whispered, her body tingling as she shifted against him. "Please, faster!"

Thankfully, Malcolm thrust faster, his hips pressing into her again and again. She arched, whimpering as she strived to reach that point. When he moved his hand lower, touching that throbbing nub, her body splintered into the most beautiful, mind-blowing climax! Ella hadn't even thought that sensations like that were possible. She clung to him, her body throbbing in a seemingly continuous wave of pleasure!

Malcolm watched, aching to give in to his own release, but also wanting to give Ella more pleasure. But she was too tight and too beautiful as she spiraled out of control and he couldn't hold back. Thrusting once, twice...and his body exploded, her tight muscles clamping around him and intensifying the pleasure as he thrust into her until it was all over.

A moment later, he collapsed against her, burying his face into the sweet scent of her neck and hair. He couldn't move. Malcolm suspected that he could die right here a happy man. No, dying would be bad because then he couldn't do that again with Ella.

Even thinking about doing this again, his body started to harden. He pulled away and reluctantly moved to the bathroom. Cleaning up, he looked at himself in the mirror, shocked to find that there weren't body parts missing after that explosion. Shaking his head at his fanciful thoughts, he walked back to Ella, smiling to find her still lying on the bed. She'd curled to the side slightly but he could still see all of the lovely parts of her. And there were many lovely parts, he thought. She only had one shoe on by this point and he wanted to roar with pleasure. His woman, he thought. Such a caveman attitude. Ella was his.

Moving towards the bed, he watched as her eyes fluttered open. There was a bit of smudged mascara under her eyes and her lipstick was completely gone. But he didn't think she could look any more beautiful than she did at this moment.

"You okay?" he asked as he moved behind her, pulling her bottom against his already increasing erection. He hoped she wasn't too sore because he'd very much like to do all of that again. Soon!

Then again, feeling her like this, cuddling against him with a soft smile on her full, swollen lips was pretty nice too.

He moved his hands around her waist, his fingers and palm flat against her stomach. He could feel her body arch against him. She was almost purring like a kitten.

"I'm fine," she replied, yawning.

"You're not sore?" he asked, his hand wandering lower, wanting to test out that area. He definitely hadn't explored that area thoroughly enough.

Ella laughed and grabbed his hand. "I'm not sore."

"Then why are you stopping me from making sure that you're not too sore?"

She smiled and pressed more firmly against him. He could feel all of her against him now. Even her legs were tangled with his.

"Because I don't think your purpose in ensuring my lack of soreness is completely altruistic."

He smiled, but moved his hand along her hip and thigh. "You might be right." He nibbled the side of her neck. "I'll let you sleep then."

She laughed, shaking her head and he loved feeling the soft tresses tickle his cheek. "I'm not sleepy."

"Your eyes are closed."

Ella grinned, but kept her eyes shut. "I'm waiting to see what you're going to do with that hand," she admitted. "If you're too tired though, then I'm going to imagine something else and maybe..."

Malcolm didn't allow her to finish that statement. Instead of the teasing touches of moments before, her words shot a bolt of lust straight through his body. Immediately, he shifted so that he was once more looming on top of her. "I don't think that I want your imagination to work that hard," he murmured, kissing his way down her stomach, his hands leading the way. "At least, not this time." He kissed his way down her neck. "Next time," he whispered into her ear.

He pulled her leg back, exposing her body to him. She felt open and vulnerable and...sexy. Wanted! She didn't have time to revel in that revelation because his fingers didn't stop moving. His fingers were... amazing! Talented, ingenious and...naughty! They teased, and flicked against that sensitive nub before moving away. One finger slid into her heat and she groaned, her hands clenching...something. She wasn't sure what anymore. She was focused on that finger, on the way it moved inside of her. When his thumb came into play, she couldn't do anything but react, pressing against his fingers and hand.

Before she knew it was happening, Ella's body shattered with another climax and Malcolm's very talented, very wicked fingers extended her pleasure in ways she never would have expected. Before she had time to recover, Malcolm had already donned another condom and slid inside of her from behind. When one climax finished, she immediately felt the next begin. It was almost overwhelming and she couldn't do anything to help him because of their positions. She was completely at his mercy. So, when the next came upon her, she dug her fingers into the bed covers again and just...rode it out until it was over. Vaguely, she was aware of Malcolm coming to his own climax as well, but she couldn't do anything to help him. Ella just collapsed after it was all over. Panting, her body melting into the bed. She felt the mattress shift as he went to the bathroom again.

Ella opened her eyes, admiring his tight butt and muscular thighs. When he came back to the bed, she might have smiled at his rock hard abs, but she wasn't quite sure that her smiling muscles were working. None of her other muscles were, why would her facial muscles be an exception?

But she did sigh when he pulled her into his arms, covering them both with the comforter as he reached out and turned off the light.

Her last thought before she drifted to sleep was that she was really glad that he hadn't left tonight. She enjoyed the warmth of his body as he pulled her into his arms, settling her against his side. Ella used his shoulder as her pillow and knew that this was what heaven must be like.

Chapter 7

Ella's eyes didn't want to open. There was sunlight streaming into her bedroom and she vaguely remembered not closing the blinds last night. But for long moments, she couldn't remember why. Once her synapses kicked into gear, forming thoughts and recognizing the world, she opened her eyes enough to look around. Something was wrong. Something was very wrong, but she couldn't think hard enough to figure it out.

Blanket...check. Her own bed...check. No headache. But her body... ached. There was a tightness in her inner thigh muscles, a tightness she'd never experienced before. What...?

That's when memories of the previous night came back to her. Sex. No, what she'd done with Malcolm couldn't ever be defined as mere sex. It had been...shocking! Amazing! Ella had been with two other men before, and the sex had been...fine. Nothing exciting. That's why she didn't want to define last night with Malcolm as *just* a sexual encounter.

Nothing that mind-blowing, world-jarring, and body-altering could be defined with such a mediocre word.

Lifting her head, Ella looked around, listening. Nothing. That's what was wrong! Wrapping the sheet around her, she looked around her bedroom. Malcolm wasn't here. And by the silence, she knew that he wasn't in the other room either. Nor was he in the bathroom.

He'd left! After the most amazing night of her life, he'd left her alone this morning? For some reason, his absence cheapened the whole night, made her feel...wrong.

She thought about lying back down and wallowing in self-pity, but that wasn't really Ella's way of handling things. Instead, she threw back the covers and stomped into the bathroom. She'd meant to take a quick shower, but the short walk to the bathroom showed her that her muscles were much more tense than she'd anticipated. So instead, she lingered under the warm water, trying to soothe the ache in her body as well as in her mind.

The water helped her legs, but didn't do much to slow her thoughts. Finally, she shut off the water and dried off, pulling on clean underwear...but not one of the pretty pieces that Malcolm had bought for her. Nope, those might just get shredded. The actions she took against the pretty pieces would be determined later, once she confronted him and found out why he'd snuck out last night. Or this morning. It had been after midnight when they'd come back from that horrible party. So everything that had occurred last night had happened today.

"You're going to have a lot of explaining to do, you jerk!" she grumbled to the empty apartment as she pulled a sweater over her head. A pair of jeans and sneakers were the rest of her ensemble...could it really be considered an ensemble? Didn't one need to accessorize before it could be considered an ensemble? Probably. So she pulled her hair up into a messy bun and plopped a hat on her head. "There!" she growled as she pulled her wallet from the evening bag she'd carried the previous evening and dumped it into her bag. As she walked out of her apartment, she grabbed her keys. "I have an ensemble." She stomped out of her apartment.

She climbed into her car and started the engine but as she waited for the car to warm up, Ella realized she wasn't exactly sure where she was going. It was Saturday morning at...she looked at her clock. Wow, it was almost noon. Ella never slept that late! She was usually up before the sun rose but also, she preferred to be in bed early. Ella was definitely a morning dove, not a night owl.

Okay, so...where did one go when one needed to vent about a night of hot, passionate sex? Cassy wasn't even in the country and Naya...well, Ella had no idea where Naya was. "I miss them," she whispered and laid her head on the steering wheel.

Ella allowed herself to wallow in self-pity for perhaps three minutes. "Enough!" she snapped and lifted her head. "This isn't doing any good. So he left me this morning. I can deal with that. I'm not some pathetic gold digger who needs a man in her life to be happy!"

Her stomach growled and she nodded. "Food!" With a goal in mind, she backed out of the parking spot and headed towards...? "I want a muffin," she decided out loud. "Okay, actually, I want a cupcake, but since I haven't had any breakfast, a muffin will work." She nodded and turned right to head towards the bakery. She lived outside of London, very close to Malcolm's, or rather, his father's estate. Which brought

Malcolm's father to mind. Where was the old codger? Several people had asked about Edward Reynolds last night.

Ella pulled into an empty spot along the village green and got out, slinging her messenger bag over her body and crossed the street to the bakery. Happily, she spotted her father sitting at a table, reading a newspaper. Stepping into the shop, she paused a moment to breathe in the delicious smells. Then she walked over to her dad's table and sat down. Immediately, he dropped his newspaper and smiled at her. "Honey! What a nice surprise!" he stood up to give her a hug before sitting down again. "What are you doing here? Why aren't you out discovering the next horrific injustice in the world?" he teased.

Ella smiled and leaned her elbows onto the table. "Taking a break from horrific injustices this morning. I stopped in to grab a muffin and spotted you through the window." She tilted her head towards his newspaper. "You know, you can get that online now. You don't have to get the ink all over your fingers anymore."

He laughed and folded his newspaper. "Of all the people to tell me not to get a newspaper, I'd think you'd be the last."

She smiled and shrugged one shoulder. "I'm a reporter, so I'm definitely an advocate for an informed citizenry. But news outlets get most of their revenue from online advertising now. Almost no one reads an actual paper these days. Online is better for the environment," she pointed out.

"True, but I do a lot for the environment already," he huffed with a wink. "This will be my one vice."

"You have only one vice?" she teased.

He chuckled. "Perhaps more than one."

"I'm going to grab a muffin and some coffee. Do you want anything else?" she asked.

Tom shook his head. "I just finished lunch," he told her and glanced at his watch, then looked at her with an expression that said she was running behind.

Ella laughed. "I worked late last night," she told him, which was the truth, but not the reason she was so exhausted today. "I'll be right back."

Five minutes later, she came back to his table with a warm muffin and a steaming cup of black coffee. In college, she'd loved those specialty coffees with the foam and the flavored syrups. But after being in Africa and the various countries for so many years, she'd come to love a good cup of strong, black coffee, savoring the flavor and richness of the beans.

While she ate her muffin, Ella and her father talked about various topics, but several times, she caught her father glancing over at Ingrid, the bakery owner. Ingrid was about the same age as her father, and had owned this bakery for at least ten years, but Ella hadn't ever noticed any romantic interest between them. Even as she watched, Ella's father snuck another peek at the kind-hearted baker, then quickly away.

"So..." she said, smiling at her father and leaning forward on her elbows. "How's your love life, Dad?" she asked, wanting to open the subject that had never occurred to her before.

Tom sputtered slightly, then shook his head. "I don't...I'm not..." he glanced over at the baker, who was watching. It seemed Ingrid wanted to hear Tom's response and Ella's heart ached for both of them.

Ella wrapped her fingers around the coffee cup. "You know Dad, Mom died a long time ago."

He looked down at his own hands. "I know that, honey."

Ella put her hands on her dad's. "Dad, I think it's time that you moved on with your life." She waited and, slowly, he lifted his eyes to look at her. "Mom was an incredible woman," Ella told him. "But she wouldn't have wanted you to live only with memories of her for the rest of your life. She died a long time ago. Perhaps it is time that you found someone new to share your life with." She paused and his eyes teared up. "Maybe someone who knows how to bake wonderful muffins," she added in a whisper.

Tom chuckled and took a deep breath, shifting in his chair. "You wouldn't mind? Your mother was a good woman."

"Of course I wouldn't mind," Ella replied. "She was great. And nobody can take her place in my heart. I don't think that you could ever replace her in yours either, but I suspect that there is some room for another woman in there. Not better, just...different. Someone who is here and can be with you. Memories are cold and can't snuggle with you at night, Dad."

He coughed, trying to appear gruff when Ella knew that he was deeply appreciative of her comments. "Maybe I'll think about it," he told her, and Ella watched him give the sweet bakery owner another glance.

Ella looked up at Ingrid and noticed that the woman was fiddling with...something. A string? Ella couldn't see, but it appeared she was trying to look busy, while listening to their conversation.

"Well, it was great having breakfast with you," she told her dad and stood up, kissing his weathered cheek. "I'm off to do more investigating." She turned and walked to the counter. "Ingrid, that muffin was absolutely delicious. Thank you!"

Ingrid blushed and waved. "Oh, I'm glad that you enjoyed it."

Ella smiled and left, waving to her father as she slipped into her car.

Where should she go now? She was still focused on Malcolm, furious with him for not being there in the morning. Had she been completely wrong about him? Had she given herself to a man that only wanted to use her? Had she just committed the unforgiveable sin of becoming involved with a person she was investigating?

"No!" she protested aloud, driving down the street. "No, he isn't like that!"

Ella wasn't sure where she was going. But she knew that being with Malcolm last night hadn't been a mistake. She had to believe that, otherwise, she might just fall apart.

She considered her next move.

Tular she thought suddenly, remembering the conversation in the bathroom last night. "What was the connection to Tular?" Tapping her thumb against her steering wheel, she tried to think, tried to remember what they'd discussed. Something about a dreary hotel in the capital and not having air conditioning? But was there more?

She'd been bored out of her mind, but Ella suspected that the conversation might have been significant. Of course, the ladies themselves were significant as well! Ella might not agree with their life choices –she couldn't imagine a career as a mistress to a stuffed shirt– but the ladies were important and wonderful and valuable. Pink Dress and Blue Dress...Ella really should have taken a moment to discover their names...were lovely women who simply needed validation. They needed to feel needed and maybe the men who paid their bills and...

She was doing it again. Ella rolled her eyes and turned her car around, heading back to her apartment. Whenever she became overwhelmed, Ella's mind wandered down an irrelevant rabbit hole. Something that she didn't need to focus on because...because she couldn't figure out the real issue.

And the issue she was trying to avoid at this moment was Malcolm and how hurt she was...devastated really...that he had left her this morning.

Wiping a tear from her cheek, she turned right, then left on the small, winding roads leading back to the village. She drove past his father's estate and Ella wondered why the old Duke hadn't been around lately. Even her father had mentioned that Edward hadn't been to several of the village meetings. In the past, the old codger made a point of attending the meetings and dominated the discussion with his blustering demands. He was still under the impression that he was the primary employer for the village and, therefore, had the right to demand concessions from the villagers.

Ella smiled, remembering the last time she'd come home several months ago. The villagers had just finished a town meeting. Some were grumbling about the duke's interference and others were laughing at how ridiculous the man was.

An issue for another day, she thought. But even as she dismissed the thought, she started considering the idea of doing a story about him. Maybe there were other villages who have the same problem? She loved her country and even loved the Royal Family. But....

Ella sighed. She was doing it again!

Turning right, she pulled into the small parking lot of her apartment and...Malcolm! He was coming out of her building and he didn't look happy.

For a long moment, she stared at him, her mind trying to interpret his expression. He looked angry but why would *he* be angry? He's the one who left at some point in the night after making her whole body tingle with happiness. He was the one who snuck out. She's the injured party here!

She pulled into a parking space and he was right there, whipping the car door open as soon as she turned off the engine.

"Where the hell have you been?" he demanded.

Ella grabbed her bag and stepped out of the vehicle. She didn't answer him for a long moment, which was probably the wrong thing to do because his temper visibly ramped up several notches.

Then again, did she care if he was angry? She didn't! He's the one who snuck away! He's the one that had made her feel special and loved and sexy and beautiful. Only to wake up feeling used. Like yesterday's trash!

"Ella, where were you this morning and why didn't you call me?" he growled, leaning over her, placing a hand on either side of her, pinning her against her car.

"Why would I call you?" she demanded, refusing to be cowed. She'd run up against brutal dictators, pirates, sex traffickers and other horrible human beings. Those people had been terrifying and she'd hidden her fear from them. Malcolm could not scare her!

Okay, so yeah, she was a little bit scared. She didn't know what he would do when angry. But no way would she let him see how scared she was.

"Why would you...?" He sighed, bowing his head slightly. "After last night?"

She shrugged. "Apparently, last night didn't mean much to you since you weren't here when I woke up. So, last night must have been just...!"

"Don't!" he snapped, straightening up and taking her hands. "Ella, don't belittle what happened last night. It wasn't just a one night stand. Not for me. And," he lowered his head, looking into her eyes, "I suspect that it wasn't for you either." He paused again, waiting for her response. "Was it?" he prompted when she pressed her lips together.

Unfortunately, not speaking didn't help because she teared up at his words. They revealed exactly how hurt she'd been this morning.

Ella blew out a breath of air, irritated that she felt so pathetically hurt. Looking up at him, she refused to lower her guard because he was saying all the right words. Words were good. Her world revolved around words. Words were her life. But actions were much more important. She used words to describe actions. Right now, she was a wee bit speechless. Unfortunately. Because she'd love to blast him with words that would hurt him as deeply as she was hurting.

"It was..." she started, but words failed her. Her expertise was words, but they weren't coming to her now.

Malcolm watched her, his chest aching when he noticed the tears. "I left you a note, honey." He wanted to pull her into his arms. He wanted to feel her body melt against his, like she had last night. Hell, he wanted to pull her into his arms, carry her back up to her apartment and make love to her all over again. He wanted to feel that oblivion, that mind-blowing pleasure. Even now, seeing her long lashes lower over her beautiful cheeks, Malcolm ached to hold her.

"Hell," he muttered, reacting to the pain in her eyes. Instead of talking this out, figuring out what had gone wrong between last night when she was a passionate, beautiful woman sharing herself with him in the most amazing way, and this stiff, angry, hurt person...he pulled her into his arms and held her close.

For a long moment, she stood stiffly in his arms. But as his hands moved over her back in a seemingly futile attempt to soothe her, she slowly relaxed. He sighed with relief, closing his eyes. "I don't know what I did to mess up, Ella. Will you tell me what I did wrong?"

That's when the trembling began and he muttered several curses. "I'm sorry, Ella," and he lifted her into his arms. "We need to figure this out." He carried her over to his car and tucked her into the passenger seat. Malcolm practically jogged around to the driver's seat, needing to get her alone and away from prying eyes. It was a small village and he was well known around these parts. Hell, his father was the village monster. Every person in this village loved gossip, and gossip about his family was a local favorite.

He'd lived with the speculation about his life and his relationship with his father all his life. But Ella didn't need to deal with that. She was special and more tender hearted than he'd realized. More tender than she let on to the world, apparently. Yeah, she was tough and hardcore when she was going after a story. But when her heart became involved...

Malcolm smiled at the realization that Ella was hurt. He backed out of the parking lot and headed for London. The tension in him released at the realization that Ella's heart was involved. That was good! Damn good! Because he had feelings for her as well. He wasn't exactly sure what those feelings were. He wasn't used to having feelings for a woman. But Ella...she was different. Different special and different important. Important to him.

Damn, he hadn't meant for that to happen. He hadn't meant for anything to happen with Ella. But after last night, he couldn't hide from those feelings. Not when they felt this good.

Okay, take that back, Malcolm thought as he turned right onto the highway. It didn't feel good to hear Ella sniff. And he hated that she wouldn't look at him. If he weren't speeding down the highway, he'd take her into his arms right this moment and explain. But he needed to get her alone, and more than just alone, he needed her away from the prying eyes of the villagers.

He hated going to that village, hated being so close to his father. It was as if there was an evil cloud around the man and, the closer Malcolm got to that old, dilapidated estate, the stronger that evil became.

Even more, he could feel everyone's eyes watching him. It wasn't just his imagination either. When he walked into the village, curtains twitched. Outdoor sitting areas of the local pubs filled up and, literally, people turned in their seats to watch him.

He hated the possibility, the probability of anyone in that village talking about Ella like that, although someone had most likely seen him carry her off to his car. Tongues were probably wagging already and the story would hit Ella's father's ears before the end of the day.

"Here," he said, handing her his cell phone. "You need to call your dad and assure him that you weren't kidnapped by me a few minutes ago."

She scoffed and shook her head. "My dad wouldn't think that."

He grunted. "Trust me, he's going to hear something along those lines. I've found that it's better to be proactive about these things when it comes to the villagers."

She'd been looking out the window, trying to ignore him or maybe just going through things in her mind. But with his words, she turned her head and looked at his phone.

"If he's going to hear that you've done something horrible to me, then he'd believe it more if I called him from my cell phone." And with that, she pulled her phone out of her messenger bag and dialed her dad.

"Ella? Honey, are you okay?"

Ella glanced over to Malcolm's, confused. "Of course I'm okay, Dad. What have you heard?"

Malcolm must have heard the concern in her father's voice because his lips quirked up slightly. Some might call it a smile, but Ella knew that it wasn't amusement. Cynicism?

"Someone came over to tell me that you'd been abducted," he announced. "You're okay?"

Ella looked away from Malcolm's I-told-you-so glance. "I'm fine, Dad. I'm with Malcolm Reynolds."

"He's not hurting you, is he? There were rumors, love. Rumors about bad things happening at his house when he was growing up. There are even rumors about how his mother died. Rumors that were never confirmed, but none were ever denied either."

Ella glanced up at Malcolm again. His face was stoic now. Good grief, what must he have gone through growing up?

"I'm fine, Dad. Malcolm is actually helping me with something. He's been the ultimate gentleman. And he's never laid a finger on me in any sort of violent or evil way. So, you can rest assured that I'm not in shackles, about to be hacked to bits and fed to dogs."

Her father groaned and Ella smiled. "You don't have to be so graphic, honey," he chuckled. "But thank you for calling. Some people around here," he paused and Ella could picture him shaking his head. "Well, suffice it to say that there are some people who need better hobbies to occupy their time."

Ella laughed, thinking about her father's gardening. It was much more than a hobby to him, she knew. It was more of an obsession. His gardening took a great deal of his time and attention.

"I think that would be a great idea, Dad," she teased, looking out the window again. "Maybe you should suggest it at the next village meeting."

His only response was a grunt. Then he said, "But you're okay?"

Not completely okay, she thought. "I wasn't kidnapped, Dad. Malcolm is a gentleman. He wouldn't dream of treating me disrespectfully."

Her eyes once again moved to Malcom. Yes, he was concentrating on the traffic, but he still reacted to her words with a smirk.

"Okay, honey. As long as you're okay," and he chuckled, "I'll tell the tongue-waggers here that you're not chopped up into little bits."

"Thanks Dad. I'll talk to you later."

She ended the call and laid the phone down on her lap, her mind spinning with all of the questions. She didn't want to ask, not wanting to invade his privacy. But her reporter's mind was going a hundred miles a minute.

There was a long silence as both of them considered that phone call. In the end, Ella couldn't suppress the questions. "So...what were the rumors that were so horrible about your family that I never heard about them?" she finally blurted out.

He laughed, shaking his head. "Other than the way my bastard father fired your mother?" he asked.

"That wasn't a rumor," she snapped back, fury returning at the memory. She took a slow, deep breath and let it out again. "Do you know why your father fired my mother? Not that it matters. I was just wondering what his justification was."

Malcolm's fingers tightened on the steering wheel. "My father fired your mother, who was a wonderful woman, by the way..."

"I know that. You don't need to tell me that because I know that."

He nodded, silent for a long moment. "She was good to me and my mother, Ella. She was a kind, decent person to everyone."

There was a mystery behind that comment. But one question at a time, she thought. "Back to why your father fired my mom?"

He sighed and turned off of the highway. They exited into the Mayfair area and Ella groaned, not wanting to be here. This was the ritzy area. The houses were huge and hidden behind either tall brick walls or elaborate landscaping with enormous yards and massive trees that were centuries old.

"My father fired your mother for the exact reason you suspect."

"He couldn't be such a bastard to fire her because she was diagnosed with cancer, Malcolm. No one is that much of a monster, although I admit, that's what I thought when it happened. And," she was ashamed of this admission, "that's what I've thought ever since. Although I'm sure the truth isn't that bad."

Malcolm turned into the driveway of one of those big, beautiful houses. "Unfortunately, that's the truth," he told her and pressed button that opened the garage door in the back of the house. One of four garage doors, Ella noted. "He fired your mother because she was diagnosed with cancer. My father fired her the moment he discovered her illness. He wanted her out of his house that very day. I remember that afternoon. He was livid that your mother had dared to enter his domain with a sickness."

Ella was more horrified. "But it wasn't her fault that she got cancer!" she exclaimed, the garage doors closing behind them. It was quiet and dark inside the garage. "Why would he do that?"

"Because my father truly was, and is, a bastard of the first order, Ella," he sighed, then stepped out of the car.

Ella followed, still struggling to understand. "But..."

"Ella," he interrupted, stopping her next objection. "He's done far worse. I don't know everything he's done, but I know enough. So yeah, he *can* be that big of a bastard."

She contemplated that as he led her into his house.

Over the years, Malcolm had made a great deal of money. He'd enjoyed the places he'd lived during that time as well. The money he'd earned allowed him to live however he wanted. And he'd lived very comfortably. But now, leading Ella through his house, he wondered what she thought of it. He'd designed it with an award winning architect but...was it not to her taste? Did she find the layout soothing?

He remembered her apartment and the surprise that it was so small and...empty. She didn't collect things. Nor did he, Malcolm supposed. But he preferred creature comforts at all of his homes. This one in London was his main residence and the one he'd put the most thought into.

"This is lovely!" Ella gasped when she stepped into the two story great room with tall, black trimmed windows that looked out onto a stone patio surrounded by evergreen trees.

Malcolm looked around, nodding. "Thank you," he replied, surprised by the relief he felt. Why was he so relieved? He'd never cared what the women in his life thought of his residences.

Then again, he'd never brought a woman into his home. Malcolm hadn't really thought about that before, but...it was true. He didn't allow the women that had come through his life to truly enter his life. He'd never had any feelings for the women in his past.

But this morning when Ella hadn't called, he'd cared. And the longer it had gone when she hadn't called, the more irritated he'd become.

"Is that a balcony on the second row of windows?" she asked, moving towards the windows that went up to the ceiling.

"Yes. I had an architect design everything. I wanted to be able to sit out on the upper deck without it shadowing the light coming in through the windows of the great room. He figured out a way to tilt the flooring so that it brought in the light."

She peered up towards the balcony above while Malcolm continued to peer at her. His eyes traveled down over her jeans, then back up to the soft cotton of her sweater that molded to her breasts. The clothes weren't particularly interesting. It was her body underneath the clothing that he found endlessly fascinating. And he wanted to peel all of those clothes off and make love to her. Right here in the sunshine!

But she hadn't called this morning. After the night they'd shared together, she'd ignored him all day long. Damn, but he hated being on this side of the relationship. How many times had he heard the women he'd been with say the same thing? Now here he was, wondering why she hadn't called. Karma was a bitch!

"I like this room," she said, turning around slowly as she took in all of the details. "It isn't one of those dark, masculine rooms that I usually read about. You know the kind, the boring rooms with all of the leather and dark walls."

He chuckled softly. "You haven't seen my office yet."

Ella cringed. "Sorry." She turned around again, looking at the large mirrors against the opposite walls that made the room look much bigger and more elegant. "This is really amazing."

"An architect and a designer gets the credit."

She looked at him with a shake of her head. "You had to have had the original idea."

"Perhaps. But we've gotten off topic."

Her shoulders drooped slightly. "The topic being your horrible father?"

"No. The topic was why you didn't call me this morning."

She stiffened and he wondered about that. She'd been so open and happy a moment ago.

"Well, I didn't call, because I woke up after..." she stammered, pressing her lips together. "Well, after last night. And you weren't there."

"I left you a note."

Her eyes widened. Was that hope in her eyes? There was a flash before it was doused again, but he'd recognized the look. Because he felt it too. For the first time today, he was hopeful that they'd just misinterpreted...everything...today.

"I didn't see a note," she argued, crossing her arms over her stomach.

"I left you a note. I propped it up on your countertop where you'd see it when you went to make coffee this morning."

Another cringe. "I don't have a coffee maker in my apartment," she explained. "Nor do I have any food. In fact, I just plugged my fridge in a couple of days ago. But I never got around to making it to the store. So my kitchen is completely empty."

He moved closer, startled. "So...you didn't see the note?"

She shook her head again. "I woke up without you next to me, and was immediately..." She trailed off. He took her hands, pulling her arms away from her body.

"Hurt?" he offered.

"No. I'd expected that." She said the words, but her eyes told him a different story.

"You were hurt, weren't you?" he asked.

Ella shrugged noncommittally.

"Would it help if I admitted that I was furious that you hadn't called? I've been pacing for hours, wondering when you were going to call. I came up with one excuse after another, trying to justify why you hadn't called. But after too many hours and too many justifications, I wanted an explanation."

She moved closer to him. Just an inch, but it was enough. "So you came looking for me?"

"Yes," he replied, tangling his fingers with hers. "I couldn't stay away."

Ella stared up at him, amazed that he'd said so much. "Why?"

"Because you fascinate me, Ella. I don't know why, but you've gotten to me." His fingers tangled in her hair and he tugged her head backwards. "Tell me that you feel the same way," he ordered.

Ella opened her mouth to tell him...something. She wasn't really sure what she might have said. But he didn't give her the opportunity. His mouth covered hers. Just a brief kiss initially. But when she didn't pull away, in fact, she leaned in, he deepened the kiss. Tongues tangled, lips caressed, and bodies shifted against each other. She felt his hands on her back and slid her own up his chest, amazed at the power hidden under the plain, cotton shirt. But the touch wasn't enough. She needed to feel his skin, to touch him and feel him respond. She remembered how powerful she'd felt last night when she'd touched him and he'd groaned and demanded more. Ella wanted to experience that again. She wanted him. All of him!

"Tell me, Ella!" he groaned when she lifted onto her toes to deepen the kiss further.

"I want you," she told him in between kisses.

He wasn't letting her get ahead of him and pulled her shirt up and over her head, dumping it on the couch. With deft hands, he stripped off the rest of her clothes and looked down at her. "You're not wearing the pretty lace pieces I gave you," he commented, sliding off the plain, cotton underthings. "Why not?"

"Because I was hurt that you left..." she hissed when he took her nipple into his mouth. His tongue swirled against it and his teeth scraped the tip, making her ache with the need to take him into her.

Ella was completely naked now while he stood in front of her with all of his clothes on. "Not fair!" she protested, but in the end, she didn't have the restraint to take his clothes off. Pushing him backwards, he sat down on the sofa and she unzipped his slacks, releasing his erection. "You're so amazing," she whispered as her fingers wrapped around his shaft. "Would you mind if I...?" she didn't finish the question, figuring to just do it instead of ask permission.

He was better than she'd though possible! Tasting him like this was amazing! Moving her mouth up and down, she tasted and teased him, felt his hands dive into her hair and wanted to laugh at the surge of power she felt.

Before she had enough, he pulled her up onto his lap. "I wasn't done," she whispered, moments before he covered her mouth again.

Ella was frantic with need, pressing against him. His strong hands held her hips still but she wasn't allowing him control like that. Shifting against him, she found him with her body and shifted until...!

"Yes!" she gasped, sliding down his shaft, wiggling and shifting until he was fully embedded in her. "Oh yes!"

Then, because he felt so good, she did it again, sliding up and then down again, taking all of him into her body, arching backwards, leaning into the interesting friction from that particular angle.

Suddenly, his hands dug into her hips, holding her still. Ella opened her eyes and frowned questioningly.

"Protection!" he explained, his voice rough with desire.

"Oh!" And she rolled her hips again. "I'm on the birth control patch."

He looked up at her, stunned and still for a long moment. "I'm clean, Ella."

"I haven't been with anyone in a long time," she explained quietly, blushing at the admission.

His hands shifted again, taking her hips in his and moving her back to his erection. "Damn it, Ella. We shouldn't..." but he still gripped her hips, guiding her movements. "I don't know how long I can last like this."

Ella might have smiled. Or maybe not. She didn't know or care. Her only concern was to ease this ache that was inside of her, to find that elusive release.

Towards that end, she pressed against him with stronger purpose. Her mouth fell open as her body tightened, spiraling towards that peak. Malcolm caressed her breasts, cupping them as his thumbs teased her tender nipples. Ella's head fell back, eyes half closed, feeling the pleasure build.

Closer and closer...

"Yes!" she screamed, her nails digging into his shoulders as she rode out her release.

Malcolm watched, amazed and so turned on, he could barely see straight. But he didn't dare close his eyes for fear of missing whatever happened next. Unfortunately, seeing her like this, he couldn't hold back, couldn't enjoy her pleasure for as long as he wanted to. He wanted...needed to...!

"Ella!" he groaned as his body took over, his climax intense and fast, throbbing into her body as he thrust several more times.

When it was all over, he held her in his arms, amazed all over again at how beautiful it felt to hold Ella in his arms.

A long time later, he stood up and carried her up the stairs. There, he made love to her again in his big bed until they were too tired to even move. They napped for several hours until they were too hungry to sleep. He ordered a pizza to be delivered and they devoured the whole thing while watching a movie snuggled up together. He was reluctant to see her get dressed, preferring that she remain naked since he was just going to take everything back off again later. But in the end, he accepted that she still looked ravishing wearing one of his shirts.

He made love to her one more time before they both fell into an exhausted sleep. Malcolm knew that it felt right to have her in his bed. In his arms.

Chapter 8

Ella came downstairs the following morning beaming. She was wearing one of Malcolm's huge shirts that came down to the middle of her thighs. She'd folded the sleeves back so that she could use her hands. As she explored his house, she couldn't stop grinning. He was here, making breakfast somewhere. But so far, she hadn't found the kitchen. She wanted her underwear and...well, he'd stripped her clothes off somewhere down here in the great room. Looking around, she spotted her clothes on the floor beside the sofa. Even as she bent down to pick them up, Ella's cheeks flared with color. It had been another magical night in his arms and she yawned, feeling exhausted and alive. How was that possible?

Ella wasn't sure and didn't really care. Life was good. He'd left a note for her yesterday. It had all been a misunderstanding...or a miscommunication? Or perhaps it had been a lack of communication. She smiled at her mental meanderings as she searched for her panties. They weren't with her jeans. Where would they have gone? Ella got down on her knees and looked under the sofa. "There you are!" she whispered and reached for them.

At that same time, she heard footsteps and looked up.

"I like the view from here," Malcolm teased, holding two cups of coffee. Ella leaned back on her heels, taking in the soft, worn denim riding low on his lean hips. And nothing else. Bare feet. Bare chest. Rough cheeks because he hadn't shaved this morning, just showered, then came down here to make them breakfast.

"You look pretty good, sailor," she teased. "I like a man who brings me coffee."

"Maybe there are a few other things that you like about me?" he said, offering one of the coffee cups to her.

Ella took the cup and then breathed in the glorious smell of the fragrant coffee. "Oh, this is good!" she sighed and took a careful sip. "Tastes perfect!"

"What are you looking for?" he asked, sitting down on the coffee table beside her.

"I was looking for my underwear," she admitted. "I was starting to think you hid them."

One dark eyebrow went up with that explanation, and he chuckled. "Why would you bother putting them on? I'm just going to take them off again after breakfast."

She smiled, her whole body warming to the idea. "I don't think I'll have any objection to that plan, but I'm just not the kind of gal who can eat without panties on."

He laughed. "Pity," was his only reply. Then he looked at her jeans. "What's this?" he asked, lifting up a tan piece of plastic that looked like a piece of tape.

Ella gasped, her eyes going wide. "Oh no!"

Malcolm's eyes narrowed. "What's wrong?"

"That's...um..." she blinked and snatched it out of his hand. "This never comes off so easily!" she said and tried to put it back onto her skin.

"What is it?"

Unfortunately, the tape wasn't working very well. It wouldn't stick to her skin again. "It's my birth control," she muttered distractedly.

There was a long silence after that and she groaned, noticing how still he'd gone.

"Is that going to be a problem?" he asked softly.

Ella bit her lip, counting back the days. With relief, she shook her head. "No! It's not the right time for any problems," she told him.

He didn't seem convinced.

She shrugged, stuffing the contraceptive patch into her jeans pocket. "I don't think so."

He continued to watch her for a long moment, then stood up. "Fine. So...how about pancakes for breakfast?" he offered.

Ella watched him move into the kitchen, confused and concerned. What had just happened? His reaction felt odd, but she didn't really know him well enough to understand his moods yet.

One might say that they shouldn't be having sex if she didn't understand him well enough. But then again, didn't it take years for two people to *really* get to know one another? And in the grand scheme of things, could two people ever really know one another?

Okay, so maybe a couple that had been married for years, decades perhaps. They could anticipate each other's reactions.

With a smile, she wandered into the kitchen.

With very precise movements, Malcolm mixed the ingredients, did a test pancake, and flipped it to ensure that the pan was hot enough. Every movement was careful and regulated.

Pregnant. The idea of Ella becoming pregnant with his child, their child, sounded...amazing.

Unfortunately, she'd dismissed the idea. In fact, she'd indicated that the idea would be bad. All the while, he was thinking about how great it could be.

No, it wouldn't be good, he corrected as he poured several circles of batter onto the pan. It was too early in their relationship for children. They needed to get to know each other better. They needed to find their rhythm. They needed to talk about having children and connecting their lives together...before Ella got pregnancy.

He wanted Ella in his life for a long time. But...she was a reporter. She was a free spirit. Ella was only in London to investigate this flaming hand...whatever. Once she'd figured out the mystery and written up her article, she'd be gone again. Off to some other country.

Okay, that wasn't fair. Malcolm traveled a great deal for his job too. He couldn't ask her to stop traveling for her job. Not if he wasn't willing to do the same. But he couldn't help thinking that having her travel with him, be with him, spend her life with him, sounded pretty damn nice! Just having her here in his house, in his bed, had been great. It felt right. Perfect.

So, how did he convince her to stay with him for the long term? How could they work this out, their two jobs, and have a family? A relationship?

Malcolm had no idea. The issue seemed insurmountable, but as soon as he thought that word, his resolve hardened. There wasn't any situation that was insurmountable. He'd learned that over and over again. Problems created opportunities. He'd figure this out, he vowed.

Although, he had to admit that her abhorrence at the idea of children bothered him. And even that stunned him. Until now, Malcolm had always been very firmly on the "No Pregnancy" side of the issue. Although, the women he'd been with in the past had probably been the reason for his lack of a desire for children. None of those women had stirred these feelings in him. They'd been temporary lovers. He'd always been careful with his past lovers to ensure that they knew that going into the affair. But there had been no conversation about a temporary status with Ella. Nor did he want that with her. He wanted...He wanted forever. She wasn't a temporary lover. Watching her sip her coffee and scroll through whatever was on her phone, he realized that he wanted her forever.

Was this love?

He didn't know. Until this moment, he'd never understood that emotion except with his mother. And even that feeling had been laced with anger towards her for not standing up for herself. To his childhood mind, his mother had allowed the duke to smack her around. Yes, Malcolm had always hated his father for doing the hitting. But he'd also been angry with his mother for enduring the abuse silently. For not standing up to him, calling the police or...hell, running away from the old bastard!

As an adult, he knew that the physical abuse was only part of what his father had done to Malcolm's mother. There had been mental and emotional abuse, which was much more insipid than the hitting. The smacks and punches had left bruises, and in some cases, broken bones. Malcolm had only heard his father speak to his mother a few times, but the tone and the words had always been harsh. Demoralizing.

So yes, as an adult, Malcolm understood that his mother had been hurt in many ways, but his childhood feelings for her were jumbled. Tainted. Everyone considered that being the child of an aristocrat and living on an ancient estate with lots of money was blissful. The reality was so much different. It meant living up to extremely high expectations set, not just by one's parents, but by the world. It also meant that he'd grown up knowing that he would have to maintain those old estates, which included buildings that were dangerously unsafe and insanely expensive to heat. They were environmental nightmares as well. In his opinion, every moldering old building on his father's estates should be torn down. One couldn't even ignore them and let them decay on their own time, because villagers tended to sneak into the buildings. If they hurt themselves, there could be a lawsuit.

Ella set her phone down. "Hey, are you okay?"

He blinked at her, startled by her question.

"Of course," he responded quickly, and tossed another pancake onto the warming plate.

"You don't look okay," she replied. "You look serious. After last night, I would think that you would be more than okay." She paused. "But after that bit of miscommunication yesterday, I don't want to assume anything."

Her words startled him. They were...good. Logical. And caring. He flipped another pancake. "I was thinking about my father's estates," he told her.

She stood up and walked over to lean against the counter, watching the pancake brown in the pan. "What about them?" she prompted.

Malcolm glanced at her at her, then took a longer second look. The light glowed behind her, through the white shirt she wore, highlighting every curve. "They are old," he replied, his eyes lifting to hers. "Are you doing that on purpose?" he asked, forgetting about the pancakes for the moment. That shadow was much more interesting. He wondered if she'd ever pulled on panties. He liked the idea of her being naked underneath his shirt.

"Old and…that had you scowling like a grumpy bear?" she asked.

"Yes." He flipped the last pancake onto the platter and turned off the stove. "I hate old buildings."

He handed her the serving platter of pancakes, then reached into the fridge to grab the syrup, butter, and fruit that he'd already cut up. "Let's eat."

"How many estates does your father own?"

Malcolm set everything down on the small table by the large windows that looked out into the garden. "It's more that the estates own him," he explained, which was the truth. "I think there are five estates now. He sold off a couple a few years ago."

"Why would he sell them off? I thought the big thing with you aristocrats was to own as many crumbling estates as possible."

Malcolm grunted as he forked five pancakes onto her plate and more onto his. "He sold them off because the old man refuses to work. He firmly believes that the rest of the world should support him because he's a duke." He spooned a mountain of fruit onto her plate as well, not noticing the stunned look she gave the enormous amount of food he'd served her. "My father rants about how the world isn't a feudal system anymore, furious that everyone isn't giving him a portion of their earnings. He's had to sell off some of the title's properties to pay for his living expenses."

"That sounds a bit sad."

"I think the word you're looking for is pathetic," he countered, pouring coffee into her cup. "He wants the world to take care of him but he doesn't like that he should have become a productive member of society."

"How often do you see him?"

"Only when we run into each other at social events. And even then, I avoid him."

"Why is that?"

"Because he's a bastard," he told her without hesitation. "Do you need to do anything today?"

Ella recognized a subject change when she heard it. "Okay, no talking about your father. Got it." She put several of the pancakes back onto the serving plate. "And I can't eat five pancakes. Two at the most." She grinned. "Girlish figure and...well, I just can't eat that much. But thank you very much for making breakfast this morning. I wouldn't have thought of you as someone who likes to cook."

"I love it. I cook whenever I have the time. Usually, I'm too busy, but on the nights when I have time, I'll call my housekeeper and ask her to get the ingredients for a recipe so I can cook. It doesn't happen often, but when it does, I find that it's a great stress reliever."

"Interesting." Ella wasn't aware of the naughtiness of her expression. "So...cooking is how you relieve stress. Anything else?"

He lifted an eyebrow. "What are your plans for the day?"

Ella's fork froze halfway to her mouth, the syrup dripping back down onto her plate as she stared at him. Slowly, she lowered her fork, her eyes widening initially, then lowering slightly as his intent hit her. "Um...I was..."

"Staying here with me? Letting me ravish you over and over again?' he suggested.

Ella nodded. "Yes," she whispered, her throat thick with desire.

He waved his fork towards her pancakes. "Eat up. I don't know if I'll let you out of bed for a while. You're going to need your strength."

Her smile was slow to come, but as images of the previous night flashed through her mind, she couldn't stop it from forming. "Promise?" she whispered.

In response, he reached over and pulled her onto his lap. "Yes. And I never break my promises."

Over the next several hours, Ella discovered that he was right.

Chapter 9

Ella rushed into the restaurant, running a few minutes later than she preferred. Normally, Ella was the first one to arrive for anything. Several times, that need to be early had helped her get the story first. In this case, she wasn't early. In fact, she was a few minutes late.

Even worse, Naya and Cassy were already sitting at the table. Glancing at her watch, she hissed in frustration, determined to tell Malcolm that he couldn't start things in the morning. Things that delayed her and made her scream his name. Darn it, even now, after a weekend of sexual bliss in his arms, she wanted to turn around and do it all over again. Even after she'd grumbled about him making her late!

As she approached the table, Naya and Cassy turned with surprise. Cassy was generally the late one. She's the one who stayed up late doing legal stuff. Too many times, she'd stayed up late into the night writing legal briefs, only to sleep through her alarm and be late for work. Ella supposed that married life had changed her.

"Don't!" she ordered them as she dropped into the luxurious chair and slung her messenger bag onto the back. "Sorry I'm late."

"You got laid!" Naya gasped.

Ella froze for a long moment, then slowly turned her head to look at both of her friends. "I...what?"

Naya laughed. "She's glowing!"

Cassy covered her laugh with a hand, her massive diamond ring glistening in the early morning sunshine. "You are," she agreed.

"Who did you...?" Naya demanded, leaning forward as well.

Ella's cheeks turned bright pink as she focused on carefully draping the starched linen napkin on her lap. "I don't know what you're talking about."

"You did!" Cassy hissed. "Who? Give us a name!"

"I'm going to have Pierce's security team do a background check on the guy. You can't be too careful."

Ella groaned. "Stop! It isn't..." she was about to say that it wasn't serious, but that would be a lie. Waking up in Malcolm's arms this morning, spending the day with him yesterday had been...heavenly. She couldn't hide it anymore, not from herself anyway. Malcolm was important. But Ella also knew that he wasn't the kind who stayed with one woman. Besides, she had a job to do and that job wouldn't happen here in London. As soon as she figured out this mystery with the flaming hand club, she would be gone, off on another challenge.

The birth control patch...the one that hadn't been attached to her body the other night, flashed through her mind. But no, it wasn't the right time of the month for her to get pregnant, she reminded herself. And besides, they'd used condoms last night, as a precaution. She'd rushed to her apartment and slapped another patch onto her hip this morning. All was good. Everything was fine. She wasn't pregnant. She wasn't in love with Malcolm and she was determined to make some headway with the investigation this week. Then she'd be gone, as would all of these confusing emotions about Malcolm. How she felt about him would be a thing of the past. All of her confusion would be soothed by distance, she assured herself.

"We just worry about you, Ella. We always have," Cassy assured her. "When you go off on your trips to find the stories, it scares the bejeezus out of us." Naya nodded her agreement.

"In the past, we haven't been able to do much, but with a man, we can help. We can put our minds at ease."

Ella stared at her two friends, shocked that they worried about her. But in this situation, she could easily reassure them. "I'm seeing Malcolm Reynolds," she blurted out.

Cassy and Naya blinked at her. The waiter arrived with a fresh carafe of coffee and the three were silent for a long moment. When the waiter finally left them alone, Cassy and Naya leaned forward. "Are you saying that you're dating the Marquis of Theeds?" she whispered.

Ella shrugged. "Yes," she replied, although she'd sort of forgotten about his title over the past few days. He was so much more than a title to her. "He's not like I thought he was," she muttered defensively.

"They never are," Naya replied. "But Ella, I thought that you suspected him to be a part of this whole secret club mystery that you're investigating."

"He's not," Ella assured them with confidence. "Actually, he's helping me figure this out. We went to a..." she searched her mind for the right term for Friday night's gathering, "well, it was sort of a fight club but without the fighting?" she offered. "It wasn't a party. It was more of a way for the rich and powerful men of the country to parade their mistresses in front of each other. It was odd. Apparently, Malcolm is invited to them because his father, the Duke, is a member of this club. But Malcolm had never accepted their invitations before, so he was a bit of a rock star that night. Everyone wanted to talk to him."

"Ugh!" Naya groaned. "That happens to Pierce as well. He's good about suppressing most of those offers."

Naya and Cassy went off on a tangent about how they ran interference for their husbands when someone tried to pull one of them into a business conversation and Ella relaxed in her chair, sipping her coffee. The waiter arrived and they ordered breakfast, but Ella wasn't really hungry. It wasn't that she'd eaten recently, but her thoughts had focused back to her investigation.

When they finished their meals, Ella leaned forward. "Can you two ask your husbands about any information they have on Tular shipments? I heard something the other night about something being shipped from Tular that sounded odd."

"Does this have something to do with the human trafficking you're investigating?" Cassy asked.

Ella nodded. "Yes, but I don't know how the two issues are connected yet. I'm still trying to figure that out. It could be a completely legitimate shipment of goods. Or it could be something more malignant. I don't know yet and I don't even have a sense yet either. Usually, my instincts kick in when I hear something like that, but I'm just not sure."

"Good enough for me," Naya told her, wiping her mouth. "I'll ask Pierce, and I'll also ask around and see if anyone else knows anything about Tular and shipments of illegal goods."

"No!" Ella gasped. "Don't do that. Please! I don't know who to ask these things yet. I trust Pierce and Nasi," she told both of them. "But other than your husbands, let's keep this between us, okay?"

"You got it," Cassy replied and Naya nodded in agreement.

"We'll be very careful," she added.

Ella's shoulders relaxed. "Good. I love you both! Stay safe!"

Naya and Cassy hugged Ella, laughing. "We're not the ones that need the warning!" Naya teased.

Ella ignored the jab, knowing that while she took precautions, nothing could stop someone if they were determined to hurt her. It was part of the job. And if Ella were completely honest, it was also part of the allure. The adrenaline rush that occurred in her job was a bit...addictive. She also loved the thrill of bringing down bad guys...and bad gals, although most of the crimes she investigated turned out to be perpetrated by men.

"Okay, I'm off to discuss my progress with my editor. He wants to talk face to face. Not a good sign," she told her friends as they left the restaurant.

Naya grimaced. "Not good," she replied. "Pierce has meetings today and I'm working on a new marketing campaign for one of his companies."

Cassy waved to her security detail, telling them they should stay back for a few more moments. "Nasir has meetings with someone in the government. But we're flying home this afternoon. You guys will let me know what's going on, right? I'm farther away, but I can be here if either of you need me. And don't leave me out of the loop, okay?"

Ella and Naya hugged Cassy again. "We've been together for this long," Naya reassured her. "We're not going to lose each other now."

Ella fought back the tears, wishing that they all still lived close enough that they could do more stuff together. But life moved forward, she knew. As much as she'd love for time to stand still, her best friends had lives to live, things that they needed to get done in their own worlds. And Ella had her life as well. A week ago, she would have been sad about leaving her friends as they went off to be with their husbands. Not envious, but...okay, yeah, she'd been envious. As she hurried down the street towards the newspaper's headquarters, she wondered about the lack of envy this time. Was it simply because she'd spent a glorious weekend in Malcolm's arms?

That didn't make sense because...well, because Malcolm was just a temporary lover. An amazing, wonderful lover, but there could be no future between them. She would be heading out of the country in a few weeks. That's all this was, an affair.

Or was it? She thought about her devastation the other day when Malcolm hadn't been with her when she'd woken up. That level of hurt didn't come from someone for whom she had temporary feelings.

"Oh no!" she gasped, stopping in the middle of the busy sidewalk. She didn't notice the angry glares as she realized what was going on in her head. No, in her heart. Was she in love with Malcolm?

That seemed impossible! They hadn't known each other long enough for love to develop. Ella didn't believe in love at first sight. Especially not with Malcolm. She'd suspected him of being a part of that secret club! She knew that he wasn't now, but when she'd first met him, Ella had been convinced that he was.

And yet...!

"No!" she said again, shaking her head as if that could stop the realization that she had very strong feelings for Malcolm. "Impossible!" she said out loud.

Lifting her chin, she forced her feet to move forward. "I'm going to be late and I hate being late," she muttered, not noticing a woman's startled glance before she hurried away from Ella. "Focus on the meeting and ignore everything else," she whispered.

Ella hurried, pushing her feelings for Malcolm to the back of her mind. She didn't have time to examine her feelings right now. She had an investigation to finish and a meeting with her editor.

Ten minutes later, she stepped into her boss's outer office. "Hey George, is he ready for me?" she asked of her editor's assistant, who stood guard outside of Jim's office.

"He's been waiting for you," George replied with a smile. "Go on in."

Ella thanked him and moved forward, pushing open Jim's office. "Hey boss," she said once she was sure he wasn't on the phone.

Jim turned away from the computer monitor and smiled at Ella. "Hey, Ella. How's it going?" He waved to the table in the corner instead of towards one of the chairs in front of his desk. That was a relief, she thought. This would be a less formal conversation. Always a good sign.

"It's going pretty well. I discovered a few new leads over the weekend that I'm following up on with my sources."

Jim nodded. "What did you find out?"

If anyone else had asked about her leads, Ella would have simply smiled and shrugged. Or probably not even mentioned that she'd discovered something new. But this was Jim and she trusted her editor. He'd helped her out of a lot of difficult situations, plus, he'd been in the business for decades. The man had sources and resources that she might be able to tap into.

"I overheard a conversation about something mysterious being shipped out of Tular. It isn't a country that was on my radar for this type of illegal trafficking, but I'm not discounting the possibility."

"Where did you hear about this?" he asked.

She hesitated. She respected Jim and knew that he was a good newsman. But she didn't want to lose this source. "I was at a social gathering," she admitted, mentally acknowledging that her reply was a bit ambiguous. "The party itself wasn't significant though. The conversations were generally boring and pointless. All but the one I overheard. So, I've gotten a few sources to ask around about it, see if they can find out anything. It might be nothing, but I thought it was worth looking into."

"I agree," Jim nodded. "Some of the best leads are the ones we don't think mean anything."

"Exactly," she replied, relaxing back into her chair. "I have some ideas on the connections, so I'll look into those this week."

"Good!" He shuffled some papers on the table. "I was hoping you could look into something else. This story might give you some good cover in case one of these sources becomes suspicious."

Ella didn't like the sound of that. "Jim, this story is huge. I don't know how big, but pulling me off the flaming hands idea isn't a good one."

"I'm not pulling you off it," Jim assured her. But she didn't relax. "This story might be connected, or it might be something else. I don't know. But I do think you are the perfect person to look into it."

"Jim, if you send me off on another story, I can't–"

"This story is right here in town. Someone came across a story about a politician that might be taking bribes. Think you can uncover the truth?" He handed her notes from another reporter.

Ella quickly skimmed the pages. "Why didn't the reporter follow up on this?" she asked.

"Those notes are from Randy Oslo. He's flying out to research possible deaths from a pharmaceutical company. He thinks that they are covering up dangerous side effects. There could be more than fifty people who have had coronary episodes caused by this medicine."

"Fifty people?" she gasped. "That's a lot!"

"Yeah. Randy interviewed several of the families here in London. They said that they'd spoken to the consumer protection agency to ask for help. The lower level employees that took the initial calls were interested in helping the victim's families. But the complaints were quashed when they reached the desk of this person," he pointed to the name scribbled in the margin. "So, while Randy goes to Canada to look into that side of things, I want you to check into this person."

She nodded, already considering areas she could investigate. "I'll check into his financials, his mortgage, debt problems, find out if he has a gambling problem. All of the usual background checks."

Jim nodded. "Good. But while you're looking into that, keep your ears open. This consumer protection agency has ties with other government employees. You might hear something from them about imports, bogus shipments, or something that doesn't add up."

"It's a long shot," she told Jim, referring to the connection to her original investigation. "But I'll see if there's anything that pops up."

"Good. Go to it, Ella," he stood up, indicating the end of the meeting.

Ella gathered up the papers, eager to get started. Her mind was full of questions and ideas. There was an area of the newsroom where roaming reporters like her could find an open desk. She opened her laptop and started her background research. If her thoughts lingered around Malcolm, wondering what he was doing now, where he was, if he was still in the city, then she pushed her mind right back to the bribery issue. Once she had some background information, she started making calls, lining up interviews with the government employees. They all seemed eager to talk to her, so by noon, she had a full afternoon of meetings.

In the late afternoon, Ella interviewed a woman named Cindy who told Ella about several consumer issues that had been dead-ended on this person's desk. Ella felt her phone vibrate, indicating that she had a text message, but she ignored it while Cindy spoke.

For a half hour, Ella took notes, but she couldn't stop thinking about the text message, wanting to see if it was from Malcolm. Cindy was quite the talker though! Thankfully, Ella got a lot of great information. "Thank you so much for your time," she said. "I know that you need to get back to work. But thanks for taking your lunch break to give me this information."

"Is the guy going to get fired?" Cindy asked, standing up and picking up her purse.

Ella's attention was raised with that question. "I don't know what's going to happen. I have a lot of others to talk to." Ella stuck out her hand. "Cindy, thank you!" she said again.

Ella watched Cindy walk away and scribbled down a few more questions. The main one, "Was the boss just unliked? Were these employees trying to get him fired?"

She picked up her phone and glanced at the message, smiling as she read it. "Dinner tonight?" Malcolm asked. Nothing else, just that.

"*Just* dinner?" she texted back.

"Feel free to use me however you desire," he replied at once.

Ella laughed, feeling a bubble of happiness envelope her. "Not love," she reminded herself as she texted back, "What time?"

He replied back, "As soon as you are finished. Text me your schedule."

She told him that she could meet him at six o'clock that evening and smiled as she dumped her phone back into her messenger bag. "Not love," she repeated like a mantra as she stood up.

Over the next four weeks, Ella felt as if she were walking on clouds. She was enjoying the bribery investigation and it was looking as if the guy, named Bernard Lingus, was difficult to work with. Ella still didn't have evidence that he was accepting bribes, but she was getting closer. He definitely lived outside of his salary. She'd also discovered that his family wasn't wealthy. So the fact that he drove a Porche to work while living off of a salary of about sixty thousand euros didn't make sense. His house was plain. Very non-descript. But he also owned a nice motorcycle.

From a distance, Ella snapped pictures of him pulling out of his garage in the shiny, new Porsche. She also got pictures of the guy trying to drive his motorcycle, but he was clearly needed more practice.

But every night, she returned to Malcolm. They always met at his place though. There was never a discussion about meeting at her place, since she didn't have any of the creature comforts in her apartment that he did.

Once a week, she met her father for dinner and he'd asked about her glowing happiness, but Ella wasn't ready to tell her father about him. For some reason, telling her father about dating Malcolm would make it real. Or maybe, telling her father would make it more...intimate somehow.

So when she went for dinner once a week, they discussed her investigations, his flowers, and his budding relationship with Ingrid, which seemed to be blooming. But nothing about her relationship with Malcom.

She also felt the need to spend the night at her apartment after dinner with her father. The night before she did that for the second time was the advent of their first argument.

"Explain to me why you can't just come back here after dinner with your dad?" he asked, lifting his chin as he shaved that morning.

Ella stepped out of the shower, grabbing one of the big, fluffy towels his housekeeper kept stacked right by the shower door. She wrapped it around her, feeling relaxed and wonderful after yet another night in Malcolm's arms.

"Because I don't get to see him very often when I'm gone. So, when I'm in town, I make time to see him."

"I thought you spoke to him on the phone almost every day."

"I do," she said as she left the bathroom, knowing that his eyes followed her. "But having dinner with him is different than talking to him on the phone. You know that."

Malcolm's eyes were hard as he looked at her in the mirror. "I don't talk to my dad. Ever. And I don't go to his place either."

That news startled her. "I know that you have a strained relationship with your father," she said as she pulled on underwear, jeans, and a tee-shirt. "But I didn't know that you two didn't see each other at all."

"Never."

"Not even for holidays?" she asked, surprised.

"No," he replied simply.

She stared at him for a long moment, stunned by his response. "Wow. I guess..."

"Why don't you invite your father here for dinner?" he asked, grabbing a towel to dry off his smoothly shaven jaw.

That stumped her. She still hadn't told her father about their relationship.

Malcolm wasn't an idiot. At her stunned expression, his eyes narrowed and his lips thinned. "You haven't told him about us, have you?" he demanded.

Immediately, Ella saw his eyes darken, but this time, it was with anger and not desire. "I haven't hidden anything from him," she replied evasively.

He tossed the towel onto the counter and walked over to the closet, leaning a shoulder against the frame. "You haven't actually told him though, have you?"

Ella hated feeling guilty. "I haven't lied to him."

A dark eye lifted in response. "So, you don't consider a lie of omission to be a lie?"

Oh, good one! "Yes. It's a lie, but..." she wavered, knowing that she was in the wrong here. Closing her eyes, she felt defeat tighten her throat. "You're right."

He pushed away from the frame and walked into his dressing room. Ella brought clothes back and forth from her place to his each night.

"When *are* you going to tell him?" he asked, his voice slightly muffled as he pulled on a dress shirt.

This was normally one of her favorite parts of the day. Second only to the moment that she came back to be with him after work. She loved being with him, talking with him. She loved feeling his arms wrap around her as she sighed at the end of a long, hard day. That moment of happiness continued while he cooked dinner for the two of them, they discussed their days, and then he pulled her into his arms and made love to her. That moment lasted until she fell asleep, sated and blissfully happy in his arms.

"Ella?" he prompted, and by the look in his eyes and his compressed lips, she knew that he was really upset.

"I'll tell him tonight," she promised, hoping that would ease his frustration with her. She couldn't even counter his anger with her own, because his anger was justified. She hadn't told her father about their relationship. And Ella wasn't exactly sure why. "I told my friends about us," she offered as he started to leave the bedroom. He paused and turned, his eyes sharp and intense.

"When?"

Ella felt good that she could honestly answer, "After that first weekend."

"So, I'm good enough for your friends, but not good enough for your father." He paused, his eyes moving over her features. "Interesting." He turned away from her and headed downstairs. "I have a breakfast meeting. Let me know when I'll see you again."

Ella stood in the decadent luxury of his huge bedroom for a long moment. Malcolm hadn't mentioned a breakfast meeting before now. He always cooked breakfast for her, otherwise, she'd just skip it or have something on the run, something he didn't deem healthy.

She'd hurt his feelings, Ella realized. By not telling her father about their relationship, she'd hurt his feelings! That realization crushed her and she felt a painful stab in her chest. Ella's hand reached up, her fingers rubbing in the general vicinity of her heart. She'd hurt Malcolm! The ache wasn't going away.

Closing her eyes, she took a deep breath. "I don't have time for this!" she snapped. "I have another investigation to look into!" she muttered. Walking out of the house, she made her way towards the garage. Her car was parked just outside of the garage, even though he'd suggested that he could move one of his cars to make a place for her small hatchback. At the time, Ella had laughed, pointing out that each of his vehicles cost about ten times the amount of her own small, economy car and it would be silly to move an expensive vehicle out of the way to make room for hers. But now, staring at her small car with new eyes, she realized that he'd wanted to make room for *her*, not just her car. He was making space in his life for her and she'd rejected that offer.

She'd rejected him.

"Damn it!" she muttered and slammed her car door with more force than strictly necessary.

Chapter 10

Malcolm struggled to keep his cool that morning. But the realization that he was falling hard for Ella and yet, she hadn't even mentioned that they were seeing each other to her father had really pissed him off. She refused to bring more clothes to his place, even though he'd pointed out that there was an entire empty closet that she could use, with drawers and shelves, places that she could put all of her clothes and underwear so that she wouldn't have to drive out to her house every day to grab clean clothes. Hell, she didn't really have that many clothes because she traveled for her job so often. Damn it, she wouldn't even park her ridiculous car in his garage for safety. Hell, he'd *give* her one of his cars if she'd take it. He didn't like her driving around in that cheap, beat up old car that must be at least ten years old. Yeah, it drove fine, but he'd still feel better if she'd drive his SUV. He rarely used it except when traveling long distances. It was a convenience, so why wouldn't she use it while she was in town?

For the past three weeks, he'd been trying to move their relationship from just an affair where they had sex, then went their separate ways, to something more. Something intimate and long lasting. Hell, he wanted her to move in with him. No, that wasn't what he wanted. His hand slid into his pocket and felt for the ring. He'd bought it last week, but because she'd rejected every other way to make their relationship more permanent, he hadn't proposed to her yet.

And now he knew that she hadn't even told her father about their relationship. "Great!" he snapped. "Perfect!" Dropping the diamond ring back into his pocket, he grabbed the reports for his next meeting and stalked out of his office, trying to banish Ella from his thoughts.

"Sir!" his assistant called out.

Malcolm considered ignoring Joan, but in the end, he knew that Joan only interrupted him when there was a problem. "What's wrong?" he asked warily.

Joan clutched the phone nervously. "It's your father, sir," he explained, holding the phone away from her ear. "The hospital just called. He had a heart attack."

"Malcolm?"

Malcolm turned, to find Ella's soft, concerned eyes.

Two feelings hit him at the same time and he wasn't sure what to do. He stood there for a long moment. It was Ella who broke the tense moment. He watched with amazement as she dumped her messenger bag onto the floor and rushed across the room to him, wrapping her arms around his waist and hugging him tightly. Automatically, his arms wrapped around her and he absorbed this moment, closing his eyes to savor her comfort.

Not that he needed it, he thought. For a long time, Malcolm had hated his father for what he'd done to his mother. The old man had beaten her so often that she'd eventually died from kidney failure brought on by repeated trauma to her abdomen. The coroner had even wanted to declare her death a murder, but the old Duke had bribed the right people and avoided an investigation.

But this...feeling Ella's arms around his waist meant that she felt something for him other than just lust. She felt sadness at the idea of him being upset by his father's latest cardiac incident. Malcolm accepted her comfort, loving her even more for it. He knew that she'd had a busy day, so her presence here meant...something. He wasn't sure what, but he knew that it was significant that she'd canceled meetings to come here and talk with him.

"I'm so sorry," she whispered. Pulling back, Ella looked up at him. "I'll drive you to the hospital so you can be with him."

Malcolm brushed her hair away from her eyes. Damn, he loved her hair. It felt like silk and he'd run his fingers through it after they'd made love every night until she fell asleep.

"I'm not upset about this, Ella," he told her, needing to be honest.

She blinked. "But your father is in the hospital," she repeated needlessly.

He shrugged. "My father and I have been estranged for more than twelve years."

Ella mentally did the math in her head. "That was the year that your mother died, right?"

"Exactly. He killed her," he told her.

For a brief moment, Ella looked as if she might argue with him. But as she stared up at him, Ella nodded her head. "I'm sorry," and she leaned in, laying her head against his chest as she hugged him. Ella remembered her mother's death and the vicious cancer that had taken her. She couldn't imagine the pain of seeing someone she loved die because of someone else's hand. "How did he kill her?" she asked, still startled by his revelation.

"He beat her at least once a week," he explained, his voice gruff and his arms tightened around her. "She died of kidney failure. It had been bruised too many times during his brutal beatings."

She gasped and looked up at him. "That's murder!" she blurted out.

"Exactly," he replied blandly.

Ella wasn't sure what to say to that. His father had beaten his mother so much that...she'd died of her injuries? "How...why was he not charged?" she asked, confused.

"Because he's a bastard who invited the local police chief to dinner often enough, and donated enough money to his campaigns over the years, that it wasn't even an option for the police to charge my father with a crime."

Ella's reporter's mind was swarming with questions. "Okay, so...do you want to go to the hospital?"

Malcolm sighed, but she realized that he hadn't released his arms from around her waist. "I suppose I should, just for legal issues. And to determine how sick he actually is."

Ella's heart ached. She loved her father and would be devastated if he even got a scrape from a rose bush thorn. "I'll go with you," she told him and stepped out of his arms. Taking his hand, she looked up into his eyes. "We'll do this together."

He squeezed her hand and she smiled, trying to be reassuring, but this was foreign territory for her. For a child to hate their parents so much was...entirely outside of her experience. There was that girl from school, Willow. Willow had been pretty, but...okay, so maybe Willow hadn't been as bad as the other girls on that hallway. Willow's father had shipped her off to boarding school because his newest wife had wanted some quality time alone with Willow's dad. Willow's father had been a bastard with a sexual addiction. It didn't matter that he was also one of the top country music stars of the industry. He'd basically abandoned his daughter.

"Come on, I'll drive."

Malcolm pulled back, laughing. "No way. I wouldn't fit in your tiny car. I'll drive," and he pulled his key out of his pocket. He turned to Joan. "Tell the hospital that I'm on my way." He turned to Ella, tightening his hand on hers. "Come on."

Thirty minutes later, the director of the hospital greeted them personally. "My lord," the man said, bowing as Malcolm stepped into the building. "Your father is currently stable, but I'm afraid that it doesn't look good. We have the head of our cardiology department treating him. She is a brilliant surgeon and is examining the Duke now."

Malcolm heard the words, but wasn't sure how he felt yet. His father was dying and...he felt nothing.

No, that wasn't true. Anger. He was angry because the man would die without being punished for his crimes.

"Call the chief of police," he snapped. "I want to speak with him immediately."

The director's eyes widened. "I can assure you, my lord, that there was no foul play here. Your father was walking outside and fell. His housekeeper and gardener witnessed the incident and hurried to his aid. They called the ambulance immediately, my lord."

Malcolm shook his head. "Different issue. Get him here *now*."

At that moment, a woman in scrubs stepped out of the hospital room. "My lord," she said and sighed. "I'm sorry, but your father is in bad shape. He's had several smaller heart attacks over the past three years, and ignored his doctor's warnings about smoking and drinking. Apparently, his doctor recommended heart surgery two years ago in order to repair two of the valves in his heart and to place stints in the others to ease the pressure on the heart. But he refused."

"I understand," Malcolm replied. "I'm sure that you've done everything you can to help my father. He's very stubborn and opinionated."

The doctor seemed relieved as she nodded. "As I've explained to your father, there is still a chance that we could save him. But we would need to do emergency surgery now. Unfortunately, he has refused. He has also refused to sign the forms stating that he is refusing medical advice." She paused. "I'm sorry, my lord, but there isn't much we can do for him other than make him comfortable. He is very weak, and is not getting enough oxygen to his vital organs. This is causing him to be impatient and short of breath."

"In other words, his body is slowly shutting down."

The doctor's lips pressed together. "I'm sorry, my lord, but yes, exactly." She shifted on her feet. "You are his heir and, normally, a person in that role is legally allowed to make decisions on his behalf, but he has papers that deny you the right to make those decisions."

"I understand," Malcolm replied. Instead of the frustration that he probably should feel, Malcolm was stunned to realize that he only felt relief. Relief that he didn't have to make medical decisions on his father's behalf.

The surgeon bowed her head with a heavy sigh, then looked directly at Malcolm. "I'll give you some privacy. If you can change his mind, please let me know. I'm standing by, ready to perform the surgery."

Malcolm nodded and the surgeon started to walk away. But Malcom lifted his hand and the woman stopped, looking up at Malcom patiently. "If the surgery was successful, how much more time would he have?"

The doctor shuffled her feet. "I honestly couldn't say my lord. I don't know how much damage was done during this last attack. And it's very possible that he's had several micro events that he passed off as nothing. Sometimes, a small heart attack manifests itself as heartburn or just an ache in the arm. Maybe a bit of indigestion. Has your father mentioned any of these symptoms recently?"

Malcolm shook his head. "I haven't heard from my father about anything like that," he said, not bothering to mention that he'd been estranged from his father for more than a decade.

"I understand," she sighed. "If you can change his mind," she repeated, but left the sentence hanging this time. It had already been said.

Malcolm looked down at Ella. The concern in her eyes soothed him. There was a deep level of frustration bubbling up in him, but not for the reasons others might think. He wanted his father alive and able to suffer for his crimes. Only one of which was killing his mother. There had to be others.

"I'll..."

"I'll go in with you," she volunteered.

Relief surged through him. He hadn't wanted to ask. After this morning, he wasn't sure where their relationship stood. But with her standing beside him at this particular moment, he knew how he felt about her without any doubt. He loved her.

Bending, he kissed her. Just a brief brush of his lips against hers, but it was enough. For this moment, it was enough. Later, he promised himself a longer taste of Ella. He'd make love to her until neither of them could move.

Straightening, he eyed the doorway of the hospital room. He really didn't want to go in there.

Stepping through the doors, he looked in at the man lying in the hospital bed. His skin was almost the same shade as the sheets. He had an oxygen tube going to his nose and an IV running into his veins. There was a heart monitor, but other than that, nothing. Apparently, he didn't want anything else going into his old, withered body.

"It's about time you got here," Edward Reynolds grumbled.

His eyes flickered open and he glared at Malcolm. But the old, rheumy eyes didn't have the same impact that they'd had decades ago.

Malcolm's fingers tightened around Ella's hand. "I understand that you've refused heart surgery."

"No surgery," he insisted firmly. "I'll be fine! I just need a bit of rest."

Malcolm nodded his head. "I understand. Ella is another witness to your refusal of medical treatment."

The man's eyes shifted, taking in Ella.

"Who the hell is she?" the old man sneered.

"My fiancée," Malcolm said firmly, his fingers tightened on Ella's hand, silently asking her to not argue.

"Over my dead body!" he gasped, obviously trying to yell. "You haven't gotten my approval to marry, you heartless son of a bitch!"

Malcolm felt Ella move closer to him and wrapped his arm around her waist. "As I understand it, you've given me legal authority to maintain the estate and your businesses, but not your medical decisions. Is that correct?"

Edward chuckled. Sort of. "Yeah, you were an ungrateful son, but you've got a hell of a head for business. Do what you need to with the estate." He chuckled. "Why don't you weave your financial magic over my accounts? I'll come out of here a wealthy man."

Malcolm inwardly cringed at his words. "So, you've run through your inheritance and want me to take over and replenish the family coffers, is that it?"

"Hell yes! You're wealthy enough for the two of us. Besides, you owe me! It's about time you took over and fixed everything." He smiled smugly, and closed his eyes. "Go away."

Malcolm glanced down at Ella. She shrugged, obviously confused by the old man's words. "Let's go," he murmured.

As soon as they left the room, the doctor stepped forward. "I heard," she sighed. "I'm sorry, my lord. If he changes his mind, I'll have my staff call you."

Malcolm nodded, his hand taking Ella's again. "Thank you," and he headed for the exit.

The chief of police was walking in just as they were walking out. "My lord!" he called out, nodding his head politely. "I understand that you asked for my presence?"

Malcolm stared at the man for a long moment, then shook his head. "False alarm. I apologize for calling you here."

"No bother," the man replied cheerily. "If there's anything I can do to help you in this time of need, please feel free to contact me."

Malcolm nodded curtly, then left the hospital, Ella in tow.

Chapter 11

Ella stared at the enormous, stone house as Malcom drove up the gravel driveway. She hadn't seen the house in years, and it looked a bit more worn than she remembered.

"He hasn't taken care of the house or grounds in forever," Malcolm muttered, mirroring her thoughts.

"Yeah, it looks pretty desolate."

He parked in front of the house and, immediately, the front doors opened. An older woman stood there waiting, her fingers twisting at the apron in front of her.

"How is the Duke?" she asked as Malcolm approached. "Will he be coming back?"

Ella watched the woman's expression as Malcolm shook his head. "I'm sorry, Beth, but he's dying and he's refusing medical treatment. So, there's nothing the hospital can do for him."

The woman showed a mix of emotions. Worry and relief were what popped into Ella's mind.

"Well," she whispered. "That's..." she shook her head, not sure what to say. "That's a shame." Turning, she moved so that Malcolm could enter the house. "Will you be needing my services if...." she stopped, swallowing.

Malcolm knew what she was asking.

"I don't know what's going to happen with my father, Beth, but you'll be taken care of. Why hasn't he allowed you to retire?"

Beth's weathered hands moved to her apron once again. "No retirement," she whispered. "Me and Harvey, we've worked for your father for...well, we don't earn enough to retire, my lord." She looked down at her feet, obviously ashamed.

Malcom took the woman's aging hand in his. "I'll arrange for a healthy retirement for you," he told her gently. "You were kind to my mother during her life. I appreciate that."

The woman's eyes widened with hope, then tears sprung into her eyes. "Oh, sir, that's...she was a good lady! She didn't deserve what your father did to her."

"No one does, Beth. He was a brutal man."

Beth pressed her lips together, but didn't reply.

Malcolm lifted Beth's hands slightly. "As of this moment, consider yourself retired. Why don't you go talk to Harvey and figure out where you'd like to live? I'll arrange for a house and an income for both of you. You've both worked for my family for more than fifty years. You're entitled to a quiet, relaxing retirement."

The woman's eyes widened further, and she sobbed, pressing Malcolm's hand to her cheek. "Oh, thank you, my lord!" she whispered, too overcome with relief to say anything more.

"Go talk to Harvey," Malcolm urged. "And don't thank me. This is only what you have earned."

The woman's trembling fingers moved to cover her mouth as she nodded and turned away, eager to find her husband.

"Why didn't she have a retirement plan?" Ella whispered.

"Because my father basically made both of them indentured servants. If any staff member broke something, they were threatened with criminal charges or offered the chance to repay their debt to him through labor. Free labor. I'd imagine that Beth and Harvey were told that they'd broken items in the household, those pieces' value was then doubled or tripled by my father's mercenary imagination, and then each of them were required to sign a confession of what they'd done with the verbal agreement that they would work off the costs of each item over time."

"Verbally?"

"He couldn't put the agreements in writing because his actions were... *are*...illegal. It's basic slavery, forcing someone to work for no wages. He could spin it however he wanted, but it's still slavery."

"That's horrible! Why didn't you stop him before now?"

"I tried. I've been in contact with Beth and Harvey over the last few years, letting them know that I would protect them and cover their legal fees if they would testify to what my father was doing."

Ella understood. "But they were too afraid of him, right?"

"Yes. Afraid and not sure how to earn a living without a recommendation from my father after so many years of employment. No matter what I said to them, they lived in fear."

Ella sighed and moved closer, wrapping her arms around his waist. "I suspect that you're going to have a lot of issues like this to tackle once you've taken over the estate."

"Yes," he agreed, holding her close. "But for now, let's see what else is going on, shall we?"

She pulled back and smiled up at him. "How can I help?" she asked.

He reached out, touching her cheek. "How about writing up everything he's done? As soon as you discover one of his atrocities, document it. Write about it. Get it all out there for the rest of the world to know about. Tell the story. I don't want anyone to revere my father. I don't want anyone to speculate or mourn his passing."

Ella's chin trembled but she nodded. "I can do that," she told him with absolute conviction.

Over the next four days, Malcolm went through the papers in his father's study, handing her anything that might even hint of illegal or unethical activities or have any reference to a club or symbol with a flame, palm or something close to it.

Ella wrote furiously, cross-referencing everything with outside information. There were illegal payments to the local police, not just the chief of police, but to several of the police officers. Malcolm gave her several invoices that didn't make any sense, so Ella got help from her editor and the newspaper's accountants. There were other issues, such as drugs and prostitutes that had been purchased for his dinner parties, a few pictures and handwritten notes that Malcolm suggested were blackmail ...the list of Edward's crimes seemed endless. All the evidence pointed to a man who considered himself to be above the law.

It was a massive article. She worked closely with her editor and the legal staff at the newspaper to ensure accuracy and to protect the newspaper from lawsuits. They tried hard to keep it quiet, not wanting anyone else to know of the breaking news ahead of time. News that one of Britain's great aristocrats, and a Duke at that, was a very bad man was huge news! It was a scoop that Ella wasn't willing to give away to anyone else.

Chapter 12

"This doesn't make sense," Ella muttered to herself as she flipped from one page to the next. Malcolm was at the hospital, talking to his father. Edward answered all of Malcolm's questions about his financial issues, assuming that his son was taking over everything. Malcolm didn't disabuse Edward of that idea, wanting to get all of his illegal activities documented and stopped. The doctors said that Edward had only a few more days, maybe a week, to live. His kidneys had already stopped working and he was living on dialysis machines. His liver was becoming toxic and his heart was barely pumping enough oxygen to keep him alive.

Initially, Ella had a bit of an ethical dilemma about Malcolm getting information from Edward when he didn't know that his crimes would be revealed. But as they dug deeper, and after a long conversation with her editor and the legal team at the newspaper, Ella realized that Edward had every right to stop talking and explaining and it was better to stop the crimes the old duke had perpetuated over the years. The man was black right to his soul, she thought as she started reading another document, trying to connect all of the dots.

"Something is missing," she muttered, shaking her head. Picking up her phone, she dialed Malcolm's number. When he picked up, she explained, "Hey, the information you gave me about the shipments on the eighteenth don't match up with the orders. Were there other pages that explained the contents?"

"They might still be in my father's study. I left several files out on his desk. Why don't you go over there and look? I'll be there as soon as I'm finished here at the hospital."

"Sounds great."

"I'll have Beth let you in."

"I thought she was supposed to be relaxing somewhere on a beach."

He laughed slightly. "She refuses to stop working until I'm finished cleaning up this mess. Harvey as well. They were able to fill in some of the blanks too, so it's good that they are still around."

"Okay, I'll bring her some muffins from the village. Ingrid makes the best!"

"I agree. Save one for me," he said, then rung off.

Ella smiled, thinking about Malcolm's sweet tooth. The man really loved dessert. And Ella loved that he enjoyed desserts as well, since sometimes, she was the dessert!

Gathering everything up into her arms, she turned and...dumped it all back on the desk before racing into the bathroom. She made it just to the toilet moments before her stomach heaved. For several minutes, she heaved and groaned as the nausea continued until there was nothing left for her to throw up.

Afterward, she sat on the floor, staying as still as possible. This was the third morning that this had happened and Ella was truly sick of feeling miserable. "What in the world is going on?" she whispered, her palm against her forehead as she tried to make sense of her body.

Then it hit her. The one word. The word that had happened to both of her friends.

Pregnant.

"Oh no!" she whispered. "I can't be pregnant!"

Her thoughts flashed back to that morning she'd found her birth control patch on the floor. It had somehow come off and...and she very well might be pregnant! "Oh no!"

She sat there for several stunned minutes, not sure what to think. Well, besides panic! Yes, she was pretty panicked at the moment! Panicked and scared!

Her hand moved to her stomach. A baby. Malcolm's baby. Her baby! Wow!

She wanted to tell herself that she wasn't happy about being pregnant. But...deep down inside, she felt a bubble of happiness. That bubble grew and grew, expanding until she felt almost light headed. Her first instinct was to rush over to the hospital so that she could share the news with Malcolm at once.

She pulled herself to her feet using the counter and looked into the mirror. A baby! Wow! She'd never planned on being a single mom, but at this particular moment, she was too excited at the prospect of this baby to worry about all of the issues that come from being a single parent. Malcolm would help, she knew that. Over the past few days, she'd come to know what a good man he was. What a strong, capable man with a very strong moral and ethical compass. No, he wouldn't abandon their child.

He'd probably propose, but she'd have to say no. She loved him, Ella acknowledged. Loved him with all her heart. She admired him, respected him, and loved him completely. But...they couldn't make a marriage work with just one person in love with the other. She'd watched her parents and knew that marriage was difficult. It was only because of the powerful love that they shared with each other that helped them through those hard times.

So, marriage was out of the question. Which only brought to mind... what did she do about their affair? It was still burning hot. So...should she break things off now? Or just continue to enjoy this affair for as long as it lasted?

She'd have to tell Malcolm about the baby, that wasn't even a question. But how? And when? After all of this mess with his father was finished? After his father passed away? Everything was such a mess right now.

Of course, perhaps she should confirm the pregnancy first. Just because she'd been sick the past few mornings wasn't absolute proof that she was pregnant.

Then again...she'd been exhausted every afternoon. And now that she thought about it, her breasts were extra sensitive lately. Last night, she'd almost climaxed when he'd touched her breasts. "Wow!" she whispered, grabbing her tooth brush and brushing her teeth, scrubbing away the horrible taste in her mouth.

"Work!" she exclaimed. "Time to work. There would be time later to figure out the baby thing."

Ella drove over to the estate, smiling as Beth opened the door. "Hello! How are you doing today?" she asked of the elderly housekeeper.

Beth's features broke out into a grin. The woman seemed to have lost twenty years from her face over the past few days. Since Edward's heart attack and Malcolm taking over all of the duke's business affairs, the stress of Beth's world had eased dramatically.

"Harvey and I are considering Greece for our retirement," she announced happily. "We found a small place in a tiny village that looks lovely."

Ella laughed and touched the woman's shoulder. "Greece is incredibly beautiful!" Ella didn't say more, because every day, Beth came up with a different option for their retirement.

"I just don't want to impose too much on his lordship," she replied, referring to Malcolm. "I won't take his offer for granted."

Ella looked directly into Beth's eyes. "You won't be relying on Malcolm's generosity, Beth. Malcolm has reserved funds from Edward's accounts, earmarked for your retirement. Although, I suspect it is going to take a while for you to accept that your life has changed now."

Beth nodded, bowing her head as she tangled her fingers together. "It is, miss. After...well, years of worrying, it's hard to wake up in the morning and not worry about the future."

"I can see that. And I'm so sorry that you had to go through so many decades of insecurity. But Malcolm will make it up to both of you."

"Bless you, miss!" she whispered, choking up with tears. Then she sniffed and straightened her shoulders. "His lordship said you needed some papers in the study. This way," and she led the way to Edward's office and opened the door with a flourish. "If there's anything that you need, you just ask me. No one else in the village knows you're here. So you won't be bothered by the local police. They think things will continue on the way they've been going."

Ella smiled. "Thank you for your discretion, Beth." Ella glanced at the desk, piled with papers. Malcolm had been forming stacks for different issues, but Ella wasn't sure which was which. "I guess I should just... dive in, shouldn't I?"

Beth rubbed her hands together, which seemed more like a nervous gesture than one of anticipation. "If you...well," she looked a bit guilty.

Ella realized that Beth was nervous, but not sure what about. "Talk to me, Beth."

The housekeeper looked over her shoulder, then back at Ella. "The thing is..." she sighed, her hands now tangled her apron. "Harvey thinks I should just...leave it. But..."

Something in the way Beth's eyes scampered over the room warned Ella that this was important! "Nothing you tell me will go beyond Malcolm and me, unless it is something we need to bring to the authorities," Ella assured her.

Beth chewed her lip for a moment, did another over-the-shoulder glance, then nodded, as if she'd just made up her mind about something. "You're looking for something," she whispered, then took a tentative step closer. "I know...places." She fidgeted nervously. "I've cleaned this house for the past several decades, Ms. Ella. And that man, the duke, he was...he did things. He did *evil* things!"

Ella's heart rate accelerated but she tried to appear calm, not wanting to scare the timid woman. "I know that. Malcolm and I are trying to prove that."

Beth's fingers clasped tightly together. "His lordship was a good man!" Beth whispered. "Malcolm was a good boy! As soon as he realized that things were bad in the house, after his momma died, Malcolm left! The duke, he ranted about the son for years, trying to trick Malcolm into coming back and taking over the finances. The duke, he muttered about bad things. He thought we were cowed, but Harvey and I, we heard and we..." Tears sprang to the woman's eyes. "We didn't do anything about them because we were too scared and we didn't know what to do. The police in the village, they came here all the time, schmoozing with the duke. And he paid them. All the time, that horrible man paid them." Her eyes glittered with angry tears. "Harvey and I didn't break or lose any of the things that he said we'd broken. But the police, they were owned by that rabid bastard!"

Ella let the housekeeper's fury wash over her. Beth had obviously been keeping things to herself for a long time. It was good that she was venting.

"I know that. He kept you under his control in a different way."

"You're right!" she hissed. "He kept the village police officers under his control by paying them. So, whenever something bad happened, the police would only pretend to investigate! You wouldn't believe all of the things that bastard got away with over the years! He paid those officers all that money, but then held Harvey and I in servitude with false accusations!" She closed her eyes, a tear sliding down her wrinkled cheek as she took a deep, calming breath. "What I'm trying to say is that, Harvey and I know where the duke's hiding places are. If you tell us..." she stopped, then shook her head. "No. I'll just...you and his lordship have been looking for the past several days. Now it's time for Harvey and me to show you everything. Obviously, you haven't found what you need in order to nail that bastard."

"Beth, no!" Harvey hissed from the hallway.

Ella turned to find the gardener staring at his wife, his face more than slightly green.

Beth's chin went up, but Ella could see her chin quivering. "Harvey, please," Beth whispered.

Turning back to Ella, she said, "Let us help you." Beth's hands fluttered for a moment, but she stood firm.

Ella took a step forward, trying to think of something to say that would assure Beth and Harvey to help. "Malcolm has taken over the duke's finances. He's in the hospital and there are multiple witnesses that heard the duke announce that Malcolm should take over. So, there's nothing illegal about you showing me anything on this estate."

Harvey's eyes moved from his wife's startled gaze, then back to Ella.

Beth took a step closer, her weathered hands pleading with her husband. "Harvey, it's time. We can't be completely free until we show them. He'll have no power after that. We'll really be free."

Harvey's Adam's apple bobbed slightly as his gaze continued to shift back and forth from Ella to his wife. Finally, Ella saw the resignation in his eyes and he nodded slowly. "You're right," he sighed.

Beth wrapped her arms around Harvey comfortingly. "It will be okay," she whispered to him. "His lordship is a good man. He'll protect us."

Harvey didn't look convinced, but his arms moved around his frail-looking wife. For a long moment, Harvey laid his cheek against Beth's salt-and-pepper hair, closing his eyes. He looked like a man about to be led to his execution.

Thankfully, a moment later, he lifted his head and looked at Ella with eyes shining with tears. "We'll show you everything."

Ella released the breath she'd been holding, slowly. Still, she tried to hide her relief, even though she felt the spurt of adrenaline fizz through her veins. This was it, she thought. Her fingers tingled, wanting to text Malcolm, who had gone to the hospital to visit his father. It wasn't going to be a friendly visit. Malcolm was going to demand answers to several strange amounts of money that had been taken from the duke's accounts. Ella doubted that the duke would explain anything, but Malcolm had wanted to try.

Ella watched as Beth pulled a step stool out of a closet, then walked back into the study. Instead of placing the stool against a wall with books, she placed it near one of the windows with the heavy curtains against one side. The velvet curtains were faded and dusty with age. Beth pushed it carefully aside and, with the press of a fingertip, a secret panel swung open. Behind that panel, were several books, journals actually. The leather-bound journals weren't dusty, indicating that the old duke had been using them recently.

"What's in them?" Ella asked, moving towards Beth to take the journals into her hands.

"I don't know, ma'am," Beth said. "I never dared to look in them. If the duke ever discovered that I knew that they were there, I'd..." she didn't finish that statement, but instead, turned and pulled a box down. "You'll need these too."

Ella accepted the box, eyeing it curiously. "Thank you," she said as Beth stepped down from the step stool.

"Show her," Beth whispered to Harvey.

Harvey's eyes widened slightly, and he glanced at Ella. For a moment, he looked like he might argue, but then his shoulders slumped, his head bowed. "This way," he said and turned, walking out of the study.

Harvey led her out of the house, Beth trailing behind them. Ella wondered where they were going, and what they would find when they got there.

Eventually, Harvey stopped beside a beautiful garden. The rest of the landscaping was well cared for, but this spot stood out as something more elaborate. More beautiful. Obviously, care had been taken to create something special here.

"It's lovely," Ella said, admiring the lush flowers and the beautiful, blooming trees that surrounded the plot.

"It's a..." Harvey's voice died in his throat and he gulped hard. He cleared his throat and tried again. "It's a graveyard," his voice barely a whisper. "*I* didn't bury them here," he told Ella. Then the man looked directly into her eyes. "But I discovered them and didn't say anything to anyone."

Ella moved closer, putting a hand on his arm. "You didn't commit a crime, Harvey," she assured him. "The duke created a situation in which you and your wife were under duress."

The man choked again. "The duke said that he'd blame me for the women's deaths if I said anything to anyone." He looked at the lovely garden. "It was all that I could do to make their final resting place into something nice." Roughly, he wiped at the tear that escaped. "I didn't even know that they were buried here until I came to work that morning." He turned to Ella. "But I'd seen the police here having dinner with the duke. I knew that they'd never listen to me and Beth." He looked at the graves again. "I did what I could for the women. But it wasn't enough."

Ella reached out, touching his arm again. "Malcolm will help. I'm writing a news article and most likely a book, Harvey. I'm going to spread the word about what a horrible man the duke was. He was an evil monster." She shifted the journals in her arms. "I'm going to prove it. With the help of you and Beth."

Harvey looked at her sadly. "Nothing is going to happen. He'll get away with it again." He sighed. "Or he'll die."

Ella clenched her teeth. "Well, if he dies, then a lot of other people are going to face the charges as well. These crimes, whatever they all are, will *not* go unpunished!"

Harvey didn't say anything more. Instead, he turned and took Beth's hands. Together, they walked away towards the small cottage where they'd lived for most of their lives.

Ella watched, saddened by the horror of what they had gone through. They'd come to work for a man and instead, had endured a decades old nightmare that only compounded as the duke gained power over the years.

"What the hell are you doing here?" Edward Reynolds barked as Malcolm walked into the hospital room.

Malcolm stared at his father, then glanced at the nurse, who looked like she was considering smothering the old man.

Edward glared at the nurse who was writing something down on his chart. "Get out! I have business to discuss with my son!"

The nurse looked up from the chart, her gaze eyes conveying her hatred for the man. But instead of scurrying away, the woman simply turned back to the chart and finished writing. Casually, as if Edward wasn't about to have a heart attack, or perhaps because of it, the nurse slowly pocketed her pen, then slid the chart into the slot at the end of his hospital bed. Then, with a look at Malcolm, she walked out of the hospital room.

"Close the damn door!" Edward bellowed. The nurse ignored him, acting as if she hadn't heard him as she moved away.

"Damn idiot!" Edward grumbled. "All the staff here are idiots!" He shifted on the bed, then lifted his rheumy gaze to Malcolm. "Okay, tell me your plans. What are you going to do to fix the mess my accountants have created with our finances?"

Malcolm watched his old man for a long moment. Malcolm didn't see the old man lying here, helpless, in the hospital bed. He remembered the almost gleeful expression as he'd left his study one afternoon. Edward hadn't known that Malcolm was standing halfway down the ornate, wooden staircase. As soon as the old man passed by, Malcom had known what had happened. As an eight year old boy, Malcolm had already become well acquainted with that look. And it filled him with dread.

Sure enough, as soon as Malcolm had raced into the study, he'd found his mother lying on the ground. That day had been an easy one. There were no broken bones. Edward had only punched her in the stomach. Malcolm had found her on the carpet, her fingers curling into fists as she slowly breathed in and out in shallow breaths, trying to manage the pain.

Malcolm wondered if the nurses were fed up with Edward's miserable attitude and weren't providing palliative care. But no, from his experience, the medical world provided care no matter how miserable the patient might be.

More's the pity.

"Well?" Edward demanded, his breathing becoming more labored.

Malcolm set the files down on the rolling table at the end of the bed. "I have some questions for you."

"Just...fix it all!" Edward snapped. "You're rich. You know what to do to make me rich again, damn it!"

"And you think I can just wave a magic wand around and fix the decadent lifestyle that you've lived your whole life?"

The man lifted his head, bushy eyebrows lowering with his fury. "Don't you backtalk to me, boy!" he roared. "I'm your father! And you've neglected me for long enough! Now fix the damn finances and maybe I'll change my will so that you inherit the estate!"

Malcolm chuckled. "Please don't. Whoever you currently have designated to inherit is more than welcome to the estate."

Edward tried to laugh. "You wouldn't give up your birthright."

"I would. In a heartbeat," Malcolm assured his father. "But in the meantime, I have some questions." He opened a file. "Can you explain these amounts? There are several payments from your bank accounts, and several more, sometimes larger amounts that are going into your accounts. They don't match up to any of your business ventures, rents, or...?"

"Don't worry about those," Edward snapped, leaning back against the pillows. With a malicious smirk, he nodded. "That's just...money someone lent to me."

"Do they need to be paid back then? What are the terms of the loan?"

"No need to pay those back," he said, waving the hand connected to the IVs. "No one is expecting repayment on those loans."

Malcolm's eyes narrowed. "So, they are illegal activities. I need names of..." He paused, looking down at his phone. He read the text from Ella, his stomach clenching. "Ella needs me back at the house. Apparently, she's found something that I need to see." Moving to the end of the bed, he looked at his father carefully. "Care to warn me of what I'm about to discover?"

Edward sniggered, shaking his head. "Don't worry. No one is going to find anything."

Malcolm's lips thinned. "I notice you *didn't* say there were no illegal activities to find."

Edward shrugged dismissively. "You're a wealthy man. You have to have cut corners or done something outside the line in order to make the kind of money you've made."

Malcolm didn't respond for a long moment. "Actually, I've never broken the law. I'm smart enough to know how to make money within it. So, I'm guessing that whatever Ella has discovered is going to prove that you're a worthless crook."

Edward tried to sit up, but his health and the tubes keeping him alive stopped his progress. "Don't you speak to me like that! You're nothing without me! You're worthless!"

"On the contrary," Malcolm countered, taking the files and tucking them under his arm. "I'm worth a hell of a lot more than you, apparently." He tapped the file folders. "I'll hire an accounting firm to look into these payments. We'll figure out what you've been up to eventually."

Edward choked. "Don't you dare! Just...trust me. No one is going to demand repayment! They're not loans, they were gifts!"

Malcolm was at the door by that point. "Were those *gifts*," he said, his tone tinged with disbelief, "reported to the tax authorities?"

"Hell no! Why would I do that?"

Malcolm shook his head. "Did you ever do anything legal in your life?" Edward simply stared back, not responding. "I guess that answers my question."

Edward glared at Malcolm. In the end, Malcolm didn't want to know. Instead, he left the hospital room, the files tucked under his arm, feeling the need to go home and shower after the filth surrounding that man.

Chapter 13

I need you at your father's estate. I've found something. Malcolm stared at the text message, trying to anticipate what Ella had discovered. Even as he wondered, he pictured her in his mind. She was so damn smart and beautiful. Once again, his hand slipped into the pocket of his slacks, feeling the diamond ring there. Would she consider marriage? Or would she see marriage as something that would hold her back?

That question, plus a million others, swirled through his head. This mess with his father was only hindering the issue even further. He wanted so much to just get the ring on her finger and have her promise him forever.

After all of this, would she ever believe that he hadn't been party to this royal mess? Would she always suspect that he was a part of his father's illegal activities? Or perhaps she'd assume that he'd simply turned a blind eye on what was happening?

With a muttered curse, he tossed the files into the passenger seat of his car and, with a fury unlike anything he'd ever felt before, sped towards his father's estate. Even if Ella could ever overlook the monstrous things that his father had done, could she ever love him? Love him, Malcolm, the man? Not the title that he currently held or the title he would inherit, but the man he was?

He doubted it. But in that moment, Malcolm vowed that he'd do everything within his power to make that happen. Somehow, he'd convince Ella to love him. To stay with him forever!

Chapter 14

"Ella?" Malcolm called out as he stepped into the old, run-down house. Ignoring the burst of revulsion at the heavy, wood-paneled walls that seemed to close in as soon as he stepped through the door, he felt for Ella's energy. He wasn't disappointed!

"In here, Malcom!" she called from his father's study.

Malcolm stepped into the room, barely glancing at the walls lined with shelves full of old books. He found Ella sitting at his father's massive desk. Short bursts of typing followed intense perusal of the books beside the keyboard.

He took a moment to watch, to take in her beauty and her intensity. Did Ella ever relax? What would she be like on a beach? While most people sat in beach chairs and read a book or dozed in the warmth of the sunshine, he couldn't picture Ella doing anything like that. She was too full of energy. Too determined to get to the next thing in life, whatever that might be. No, Ella was too intense to relax on a beach. He couldn't picture her dozing or reading, but he could picture her diving into the surf, trying to outrun a wave. Body surfing or swimming out past the waves to see how far she could go, then coming back, as if racing some demon over her shoulder, then walking up the beach laughing because she'd either won or lost, whichever was in her head.

She was so damn beautiful! And so filled with energy. He wanted that energy! He wanted to hold her and feel her body press against his. But he also wanted to see where her energy and determination would lead them.

"What did you find?" he asked, smiling despite his memories of this room. With Ella in here, the bad memories were held at bay. He could simply look at her and know that there was good in the world.

"Malcolm!" she gasped, as if she'd forgotten that she'd just called out to him, letting him know that she was in here. He almost laughed, but then paused because he wasn't sure how long he'd stood here in the doorway watching her.

"I just came from the hospital," he said, not sure what relevance that had at the moment.

She blinked, then tilted her head. "Your father is still hanging on?"

Malcolm pushed away from the doorway. "*Edward* is still alive," he clarified, preferring to distance himself from the old man, refusing to acknowledge the relationship.

She seemed to understand. "Right. Well, come here and look at this. Beth trusted me enough to show me Edward's secret hiding place for his journals. He didn't keep things on his computer, like most people these days. There's a secret panel over there by the window," she told him, waving her hand towards the middle window. "And I've just started going through it all. Edward had a code, but it wasn't particularly difficult to figure out his system. Here's what I've found so far," she said, pointing to a spreadsheet.

Malcolm came around to the other side of the desk –an area that had previously been forbidden to him, as it was the place where Edward reigned supreme– and looked at the old journals spread out on the desk. Some were accounting journals, more like ledgers, and others looked like diaries, but as he skimmed through a couple entries, he realized they were explanations for the man's crimes over the decades.

"He actually wrote this stuff down?" he asked, incredulous as he leaned forward, looking more intently at the information scrawled with Edward's personal handwriting. The page currently displayed detailed a blackmail scheme for...Malcolm looked up at Ella, stunned. "He blackmailed the prime minister?"

Ella sat back in the enormous leather chair. "Not the current one," she clarified. "It appears that Edward was even worse than we'd thought." She flipped through several other pages. There were lists of illegal shipments containing animals, humans, drugs, and even a few arms shipments. But there was also a notation that Edward didn't like the arms shipments because the power wasn't in his favor. Another page detailed bribes to government officials, both in London as well as in countries all over the world.

"We're going to have to cross reference these amounts against his bank accounts," Malcolm commented grimly. "I'll get my accounting staff in here to help. They can work on the financial end of things, while we work on the details." He turned and looked down at her, then couldn't resist pulling her into his arms. "Damn, Ella! What have you uncovered?" he breathed, resting his cheek on the top of her head as they stood there, stunned by what they had found.

"It's pretty bad," she agreed.

Over the next three weeks, Ella worked with Beth and Harvey at the estate while Malcolm hired a private accounting firm. At the advice of his legal team, the private accounting firm would keep everything separate from Malcolm and his private businesses, just so that there was no possibility of anyone associating his efforts at unraveling Edward's misdeeds with Malcolm's more legal businesses. This way, no one could claim that Malcolm hid anything once Ella's story was published.

They worked side by side to piece together the details of Edward's crimes during the daytime hours, but as soon as the sun set, Malcolm would collect Ella, lock everything up, and take her back to his place.

He wouldn't touch her immediately though. Not until they'd both showered. It wasn't a question for either of them. They simply stepped into his large, light-filled house...so completely different from Edward's dark and heavy estate...and both of them silently headed up the stairs to the huge shower in the master bedroom, needing to wash off the smell of Edward's crimes.

But as soon as they were both clean, Malcolm took her into his arms and made love to her. Sometimes, he took her slowly, kissing every inch of her until she was writhing beneath him, screaming out for him to give her that beautiful release. And other times, they couldn't wait. She'd grab him and kiss him. He'd lift her into his arms and set her down on the bathroom countertop, taking her there, fast and furious. Sometimes, they didn't even make it that far. The wall of the shower was closer and their need to touch and explore, to surge towards that blissful release, was more important than a horizontal surface.

Some nights, after they'd made love and eaten, satisfying all of their hungers, both of them would work a bit longer. Ella was frantic to get the story written as quickly as possible. There was the fear that someone else would discover the criminal activities that Edward had perpetrated over the years, and Ella wanted that scoop. She wanted to be the one to bring it to the world. But there was also a sense of closure. So many crimes needed to be punished. And until they worked through all of the details, discovered all of the officials that had taken bribes over the years, they couldn't go to the authorities. Their concern was that one of those unethical officials would sweep all of the crimes under the rug.

Three weeks into their discovery, Ella leaned back against the deep cushions of Malcolm's sofa, watching him. He was working at his desk, set up off to the side of the magnificent room. She smiled, noticing the crease between his eyes as he worked. He was holding bank statements, using a pencil to tick off line items as he cross checked them against something in the journal.

She shivered, thinking about the way he'd touched her earlier that night. He was such an amazing lover. He seemed to find a new place to touch her every time they came together, a place that sent shivers with need through her body.

Would this intense craving for him ever ease up?

She caressed her stomach. Yes, she was positive that she was pregnant now, although thankfully, the morning sickness had eased up. There were still mornings when she moved a bit more slowly than usual, she hadn't had a period in too long, her breasts were extremely tender, and...and she craved black beans. She'd never really liked them before, but now, she couldn't seem to get enough of them. She even bought some black bean burgers, which they'd eaten for dinner this evening. Malcolm had only lifted an eyebrow when she'd taken the package out of the cotton grocery bag. But he'd heated them in the oven, while she cut up lettuce, tomato and onions for their "burgers".

"I love you," she whispered. Not loud enough for him to hear her. Ella knew that he wasn't in a place where he could handle that kind of a revelation from her. Nor did she believe that he loved her back. So, Ella hugged her feelings close to her heart, ignoring the slight pang at the idea of leaving him when this was all over.

She needed to tell him about the baby, she thought. Ella kept looking for the perfect time to tell him. But it never seemed to come. They were so busy with this investigation and discovering everything they could. And yet, was it fair for her to know something so important and keep that news from him?

No, it wasn't.

She needed to tell him. Now! Tonight!

"Malcolm, I need ..." The phone rang. He glanced at her, and then at the phone. It was after ten o'clock at night, it had to be important.

"Reynolds," he snapped when he lifted the phone. His lips tightened and he leaned back in the chair, sighing as he rubbed his forehead. "Yes. Fine. If he's agreed to the surgery, then that's fine."

There was another long pause, then Malcolm hung up the phone.

"Your..." she paused and corrected herself. "Edward agreed to the heart surgery?" She saw the truth in Malcolm's eyes.

"Yes."

She didn't say anything. Instead, Ella stood up and walked over to him, curling up in his lap. She felt his arms go around her, tightening almost painfully. No words were spoken. She didn't understand what he was feeling and Ella suspected that he didn't either. That was okay, she thought as she turned to kiss his neck, then tightened her arms around him when she felt his shudder.

Chapter 15

Edward Reynolds recovered from heart surgery with astounding speed. In fact, he was shouting at one of the nurses when Ella's news story was released into the world. The timing was perfect, the entire nursing staff was beaming when the police came by to handcuff him to the hospital bed.

"What the hell do you think you're doing?" Edward demanded. "Malcolm, call my attorney!" he roared when he spotted Malcolm standing by the doorway.

"I'm sorry, Edward, but a judge has frozen your bank accounts. Your attorneys requested that you find alternative representation." Malcolm tossed a newspaper onto his father's lap. The headline screamed "Duke of Theeds a Human Trafficker!"

What little color there was drained from Edward's face as he touched the newspaper with his free hand. "What have you done?" he whispered hoarsely.

Malcolm didn't bother to explain. Instead, he stepped out of the room as a judge and a public defender stepped into the hospital room. Because of the seriousness of the reports, as well as the mountain of evidence that Ella's editor sent to the authorities, the courts had sent over representatives to the hospital. The judge did a bail hearing right there in the hospital room. It was deemed by the hospital doctors that Edward Reynolds was healthy enough to be transferred to the prison hospital, where he would be remanded into custody until his trial.

The public defender, one of the newest members of the system who had been assigned to represent the aging aristocrat since no other legal representative was willing to touch the case, was mostly ineffectual against the arguments of a much more seasoned prosecuting attorney.

Malcolm watched with stoic interest when the nursing staff hurried to open the hospital doors as the old man was wheeled out of the hospital room on a gurney. After the blustering, furiously outraged old man was pushed out, a strange silence descended on the cardiac floor. And then there was a burst of applause. Malcolm turned, watching with a slight curve to his lips as Ella walked onto the floor.

The entire hospital floor, nurses, doctors, visitors and even some of the patients, recognized her from the byline that had accompanied the story this morning. Everyone applauded, cheering for Ella.

Malcolm chuckled softly when she stopped, stunned by the staff's reaction. An adorable blush bloomed in her cheeks, and she smiled shyly. It was such a dramatic change from her normal "charge-through-life" demeanor...and he loved her all the more for it.

She was such a complex woman, and yet, so simple as well. He touched her, she sighed with pleasure. She beamed up at him, the love she felt for him shining in those glorious eyes of hers, and his love for her increased by the moment.

For decades, he'd gone through life knowing that his father hated him and his mother wasn't capable of loving him through the agony her life had become. So feeling Ella's love was like a balm to his wounded soul.

And damn it, he loved her so much! Everything about her was like a freaking aphrodisiac. Her smile, her curves, her energy, and her gentleness. Even right now, he wanted her. He wanted to scoop her up into his arms and carry her to a private place where he could make love to her, show her how much he loved her. It wasn't enough that he knew they would make love tonight. He needed her now!

"I need to talk to you," he murmured as the cheers and applause slowed.

"Your...Edward was arrested?" she asked as he took her elbow, leading her out of the hospital.

"Yes. You passed him, didn't you?'

"Yes. But...how are you feeling? I know that..."

"I don't care about him, Ella. I'm relieved that justice is finally coming to him. I'm relieved that he wasn't going to escape punishment for his crimes." He pushed a button, calling for the elevator. But it didn't arrive fast enough. Looking around, he spotted the stairway and gently, but urgently, tugged her through the fire doors. When they were alone, he pulled her into his arms and pressed her back against the wall, kissing her as if his next breath depended on it. And it was entirely possible that it did!

Thankfully, she kissed him back, wrapping her arms around him. Even that simple gesture, the acceptance of his feelings for her, even though those feelings were cloaked in action instead of words, sparked his need for this woman higher. He felt an almost insane need to possess her, to announce to the world that this amazing, dynamic, energetic and crazy woman was his. All his!

Pulling back, he noticed that her breathing was just as erratic as his. "Let's go," he said, taking her and leading her down the stairway.

"Malcolm," she said, and he slowed when he felt her tugging on his hand. "Malcolm, we really need to talk."

"I know. I've needed to tell you something for a while now," he said to her, and kept pulling her down the stairs. They came to the lobby and he pushed out of the stairwell. Unfortunately, that meant that they were now surrounded by people rushing around. It was too busy here for him to kiss her again and he also knew that she was a celebrity today. After the astounding news article, everyone seemed to recognize her. Even as they walked through the lobby, he noticed several people point in her direction.

He wanted to kiss her again, just to show her how proud he was of her efforts. But the need to show her was private too.

"I'm parked over here," he clicked the locks to his car. She dove into the passenger seat and he circled around to the driver's side. As soon as they were safe in the relative privacy of his car, he turned to face her.

"Malcolm, we *really* need to talk!" she whispered, putting a hand to his shoulder.

"I know," he replied, then chuckled.

"Malcolm, I'm pregnant!" she blurted.

He heard the words, but because he'd been inches from kissing her again, his finger wrapped around the diamond ring in his pocket, it took him several seconds to change gears.

"You're pregnant?" he repeated, waiting for the words to compute.

Ella swallowed, looking down at her fingers on her lap. "Yes. I think I'm about seven weeks along," she admitted. "I know that I should have told you. But the timing never seemed right."

She peered at him, trying to determine what he was thinking. But his eyes were skimming the parking lot, silently asking, "This was the right time?"

"I know!" she burst out, unable to look him in the eye any longer. "I know that this is the worst possible moment. Edward was just arrested, the news just came out about everything he'd done, and...well, I just couldn't wait any longer. It wasn't fair of me to keep this to myself." She lifted her head, staring straight out of the windshield. "I just...I wanted..."

"Marry me."

Ella blinked and turned to look at him. Then she looked down at the sparkling diamond ring he held with his thumb and forefinger. Ella was speechless.

"Marry me, Ella." She stared into his blue gaze. He looked so intense, so sincere. For a brief moment, Ella allowed herself to feel the intense joy at his words.

But then reality came crashing down around her, just as it always seemed to. "I can't!" she whispered.

There was another stunned moment, and he asked, "Why?"

Ella hiccupped as the tears raced down her cheeks. "I love you, Malcolm." She lifted her eyes to look at him, needing him to see the sincerity there. "I love you so much!" She lifted her hand to stop his next words. "Please, let me finish." She sniffed, then wiped the tears away with the back of her hand. "I love you and I know that I will always love you, Malcolm. But right now, you're on an emotional roller coaster. You don't want to marry me, Malcolm. Not really. You've just witnessed your father being arrested and he will go to prison for everything he's done. And you've just been told that you're going to be a father." Another sniff. "But you don't love me. I know this, and I respect your honor in proposing to me. That's exactly what I knew that you'd do because you are so honorable. But I love you too much to trap you into a marriage that you'll regret later." She took his hand, ignoring the diamond ring he was still holding and looked into his eyes, blinking rapidly to see him clearly through the haze of tears.

"I love you so much. Too much to marry you. But we'll raise this child together. We'll do the co-parenting thing and we'll make sure that we do it right. You'll be the best father! I know that you will! And I know that you'll find someone that you'll love to marry. I'm the one that took down your family, so I know that it can't be me. But eventually, you'll marry and we'll work that out too. Our baby will be so loved!" She swiped ineffectually at the tears pouring down her face and sniffed. "We'll work it out! I just...I won't make it awkward either. I love you too much to do that to you."

With that, she jerked at the door and stepped out of his car. With a burst of energy, she ran away, back into the busy hospital and lost herself in the crowd. It took her another half hour to find her own car. The tears didn't help, but thankfully, it wasn't an odd sight to see a woman sobbing in a hospital hallway, so no one stopped her.

Ella knew that she'd never be okay again.

Chapter 16

Malcolm drove home in a fury, ready to beat something. Preferably Ella's adorable ass. But Ella wasn't at his house. Nor was she at her apartment. He banged on her door several times, but there was only silence in response. Too silent. Ella was too full of energy for that kind of silence.

Turning around, he glared at the parking lot. Her car wasn't there, so he turned and drove back out, heading towards her father's house.

"Is she here?" Malcolm demanded as soon as Tom opened the door.

Tom's startled expression revealed the truth even before the older man replied. "No! I haven't seen Ella since early this morning. She stopped by to warn me about the news article and..." Tom paused, concerned. "Are *you* okay? I mean, the news...it said that you cooperated, that you were instrumental in helping with the entire investigation but..."

Malcolm had anticipated this. "My father was a bastard of the first order. His arrest has been a long time coming. So yes. I'm more than fine. I'm relieved, actually." He leaned in closer. "Please, if you see Ella, tell her that I need to talk to her."

Tom nodded. "I will," he replied, but he was talking to air since Malcolm had headed back to his car, speeding away in his need to find her.

Three days later, Malcolm still couldn't find her and he was livid! How dare she tell him that she was pregnant...with his child!...and that she loved him then walk, no, run away from him! She hadn't answered his calls, hadn't responded to his texts. He couldn't find her anywhere, her editor probably knew where she was or, at the very least, how to contact her, but that bastard wasn't talking.

Malcolm hefted the glass of scotch in his hand, and set it down. He didn't want to drink. He wanted to find Ella. Standing here in his house, which had seemed so perfect for him before, but now felt...empty, he cursed the world.

"Where the hell are you, Ella?" he whispered. Unfortunately, the dark night didn't answer.

He worried about her, wondering if she was eating properly. She was so intent on conquering the world, she often forgot to eat. He wanted to cook for her, for their baby, to hear how she was feeling and hold her in his arms. He needed her energy and her smiles. He needed...!

Damn it, he needed her! He needed all of her!

And a baby? Hell, he'd never thought about being a father before. But yeah, the idea of Ella being pregnant, of her being pregnant with his child...with their child...was pretty damn amazing!

Now he just needed to find her and tell her that he loved her!

Chapter 17

"Ella, you can't go on like this," Cassy announced, sitting down next to Ella on the bench in the courtyard.

Ella sighed, looking up at the sunshine. "I know," she whispered, then looked down again. "I know."

Cassy wrapped a comforting arm around her shoulders. "Hey, did you hear that your newspaper is awarding you some big thing this weekend?" she teased.

Word had come out that Ella had been nominated for another Gemstone Award, but their paper had jumped the gun and was honoring her at some huge banquet. Her story about Edward Reynolds had resulted in the arrest of twenty government officials and had stopped a major sex trafficking ring. In fact, her investigation had uncovered the locations of thirteen different buildings where young women and a few men had been housed and parceled out for prostitution. More than sixty-five women and four men had been rescued. The families of the two women who had been murdered and buried on the estate in that lovely garden had found closure, although neither had moved their daughters from their final resting places once they'd seen what Harvey had done to their grave sites.

"Yeah. My editor ordered me to attend," she replied, sighing with resignation. "I need to get back out there. And I need to find another story to investigate."

Cassy laughed. "You need to find a bigger apartment," she teased, patting Ella's mostly-flat stomach. "You're ten weeks along, but time flies." She laughed, shaking her head. "Time flies during the pregnancy until the last two weeks. Then the seconds tick by so slowly, you'll want to stomp on any clock that you pass!"

That got a small smile from Ella, but it quickly disappeared. "I just..."

"You want Malcolm," Cassy replied, understandingly.

Ella inhaled slowly, trying to stifle the pain she felt whenever she thought of Malcolm. Finally, she nodded. "Yes. I want Malcolm. But...I don't think he loves me." She bowed her head. "After everything he's had to endure, Cassy, I don't think he knows *how* to love."

Cassy looked out at the courtyard as well, appearing to ponder that comment. "I think that you're not giving him enough credit, Ella."

"No, you don't understand. His father was horrendous."

"I know. I read your story."

She smiled, feeling a warmth at her friend's words. It quickly dissipated as Malcolm's stunned expression came back to her. "He said that he hates his mother at times."

"Because she didn't run away. You told me."

Ella sniffled. "I sound pretty pathetic, aren't I?"

"Yep," Cassy said, nodding for emphasis. "Which is weird. Very unlike you."

Ella laughed, loving Cassy for bringing humor into the conversation. "I know. I need to..."

Cassy took Ella's hands in both of hers. "You need to go to this awards ceremony, Ella. I'm coming with you and Naya is meeting us in London. We'll all be there for you. But you gotta go."

Ella knew that her friend was right. And in truth, she was sick of hiding here, feeling pathetic. "You're right. I need to get back to work." She turned and faced Cassy again. "Thank you for letting me hide here for a while. I needed to get my head on straight."

Cassy stood when Ella did and they linked arms as they made their way back into the palace. "What are you going to say to Malcolm when you see him again?"

Ella shrugged. "I'm sure that we'll work out a sensible plan for the baby. He'll want to be involved. He's honorable like that."

"I suspect that he'll want to be more than just involved," Cassy squeezed her arm.

Ella had no idea what that meant, but as soon as they stepped into the palace, they were confronted by her husband, a small army of guards, and an impressive mountain of luggage. "We're leaving now?"

Cassy grinned. "No time like the present!"

Ella knew Cassy was right. It was time to get back into the world of the living. Hiding out here had been fine. She'd needed the break from the scrutiny caused by the news article. Her editor had even advised her to take a vacation for a while. Because of the news about Edward Reynolds and all of the additional arrests and subsequent investigations, her name and picture were constantly in the news. She couldn't investigate any new stories yet because she was just too recognizable right now.

Chapter 18

"Is she with you?" Malcolm demanded into the phone, as he paced the wood floors of his house.

"She's with me," Nasir assured him.

"Is she okay? Is she eating?"

Nasir laughed softly. "She's fine. My wife has been taking excellent care of her and I have extra security with me to protect her. Malcolm, I promise that I will get her to you soon."

Malcolm ran a hand over his face, knowing that Nasir would do the right thing, but Malcolm wanted to be there for Ella! "She's mine to take care of! She never should have run away! Why the hell did she do that?"

"I suspect that you already know why, and the question was rhetorical."

Malcolm closed his eyes again. "Just...get her back here safely, okay?"

Another deep laugh. "We land in twenty minutes and I guarantee that she'll be at the awards ceremony tonight."

"Thank you!" Malcolm replied with heartfelt sincerity.

Even after his friend's assurance that Ella was okay, he still paced back and forth. He was already dressed in a damned tuxedo and he'd chosen the gown for Ella to wear tonight. It had been delivered to Nasir's place earlier this afternoon.

Taking a deep breath, he vowed to be calm and controlled when he saw her tonight. He would simply explain that he loved her and coax a vow out of her that she'd never leave him again.

Chapter 19

"Stay close to her tonight," Nasir warned his security team. Turning to Ella, he explained, "You've been out of the public eye for a while. Everyone is eager to see you. There is a larger than usual crowd waiting for your arrival at the hotel, so my guards will remain by your side until they are no longer needed."

Ella's eyes widened. "Why would...?" She stopped, remembering something her editor had said. "Interviews," she groaned. "I should have stayed and done the stupid interviews! Then all of this would have died out by now."

"Possibly," Cassy replied, adjusting one of Ella's curls. "You look beautiful, by the way."

"Thank you." She let her hand drift over her slightly curved tummy. "I feel different."

Cassy grinned. "Pregnancy will do that to you."

A half hour later, Nasir's driver pulled up outside of the hotel where the awards ceremony would take place. There was a large crowd that started jumping up and down when they realized that Ella was about to step out of the SUV. The screams of excitement were almost deafening and Ella felt two strong men take their place on either side of her.

"You're amazing, Ella!" someone yelled. There were more calls and signs lifted over everyone's heads saying that she was a national hero, that she'd struck a blow for women everywhere, and other signs that she couldn't read because of the camera's flashing in her eyes.

"We're here for you," one of the guards murmured in her ear. "Just walk forward."

Ella walked forward, grateful for their help. They were wearing sunglasses, obviously having anticipated this craziness. She lifted a hand to wave at the crowd of people cheering her name as she walked into the hotel.

Inside, she sighed with relief, but that feeling was short lived as another crowd moved towards her as soon as they recognized her. This was a more elite crowd, but there were so many people who wanted to shake her hand, ask her questions, offer her additional news stories to investigate, job offers, and so many other offers that she wasn't sure what to say or do.

"I've got ya," a deep voice said close to her ear.

"Malcolm!" she gasped, automatically turning to look up at him as he wrapped an arm around her waist. "You're here!"

He nodded to the guards who immediately started clearing a path. "I'm here, and I'm so furious, you should be terrified."

Ella laughed. "You wouldn't hurt me," she replied with absolute conviction, leaning into his arm.

"Want to bet on that?" he growled, but his breath caressed her ear, causing her to shiver with awareness. "We're going to talk. Now!"

He led her into one of the small offices for the hotel, shutting the door and closing out the sounds of the insanity.

"Now!" he snapped and turned to face her.

Ella stepped backwards, surprised by the fury in his eyes. "Malcolm?"

"Let's get one thing straight right now," he growled, advancing on her. "You will *never* say something like that and then leave me, ever again. Clear?"

"That I'm pregnant?"

He waved that away. "We'll get to that in a minute. I'm talking about the other thing."

"That I'm in love with you?"

"Yes! You said you love me, then you ran away! What the hell was that about, Ella?!"

"Well, I just..."

"I don't care what you 'just' thought, Ella! I love you too! But you didn't give me a chance to reply, did you? In fact, you dismissed my feelings, told me that I *didn't* love you! You made up your mind about me, without giving me a chance!"

Ella realized that he was truly furious. "Malcolm, I didn't..."

"You created this whole scenario in your mind because you're too afraid of what might happen if I did love you. If we loved each other!"

"I'm not afraid of anything!"

"Really? Then why did you run away? Admit it, Ella. You're afraid of being hurt, like your father who was devastated when your mother died. So you came up with this ridiculous idea that I can't love you, which made everything safe. Because then we couldn't be in a real relationship. That meant you were safe from being hurt."

"I *was* hurt!" she yelled back, furious that he didn't know how she felt about him. Unfortunately, his comments resonated with her. Had she run away because she was afraid that he might love her? In a weird way, it made sense.

"You run away from everything. It's one of the reasons you prefer investigating issues in foreign countries, isn't it? Because you know that you'll never fall in love with someone committing a crime. You're safe. You don't have to invest in a real relationship. You don't have to truly learn to live and love and form a life with someone who might leave you eventually."

"I...!" Ella realized that she couldn't argue. He was right! She'd never thought about it like that before. But he was absolutely right! Unfortunately, she was too stubborn and moved on to her backup issue. "Yes, well, I'm not marrying you because I'm pregnant!" she said, feeling a bit better that she had that to throw at him.

His eyes turned harder. "Seriously? Ella! Don't go there!"

"It's true! You're honorable, Malcolm. You'd marry me just because I'm pregnant!"

She tried to slip away from him, but he was close enough now that he could reach out and grab her arms, stopping her retreat. "Ella! Think about it! I had the ring! I'd already bought the ring! You'd told me about the pregnancy that day, but I already had a ring in my hand, already knew that I wanted you for the rest of my life!"

Darn it, she hadn't thought about that! "Yes well...!"

"Stop!" he snapped. "Just stop! No more telling me what I feel or don't feel. No more trying to dismiss my honor! Tell me straight Ella. I love you. You love me. Are you too afraid of risking life and whatever might come at us? Are you going to marry me? Because I'm ready to toss you over my shoulder and...!"

He didn't have a chance to finish his statement because she covered his mouth with her fingers. "I'm not afraid of anything!"

"Good!" he retorted, pulling the ring out of his pocket. He didn't give her a chance to pull away before he'd slid the ring onto her finger. "Then we're engaged. And Ella, let me just warn you that we're getting married *tomorrow*! I'm not risking you running away from me again!"

Ella stared at the ring, her heart pounding heavily against her ribs. "Malcolm, what if...!"

He heard the terror in her voice and pulled her close, wrapping his arms around her. "Ella, if something happens, we'll face it together. Just as we faced my father's crimes. We did it together."

The trembling came with his words and she closed her eyes. Her fingers curled around the ring, wanting to shield her heart from his claims. But her heart was weak and was pounding too hard, too excited at the prospect of spending her life with him.

"Okay," she whispered.

His arms tightened around her with that agreement. "Promise?"

She laughed, but it was a hiccupping sound. "Yeah. I promise." With that assurance, he kissed her long and hard, sealing her promise.

"Good. Let's get out there and do this." He took her hand and led her out of the office. With one hand on the doorway, he looked back at her. "I'm warning you now though. We're not staying late tonight. You'll get the award, then..." he trailed off.

"What?" she asked, her fingers clenching around his. "What's wrong?"

"You're pregnant!" he whispered. He dropped to his knee so that his face was eye level with her slightly rounded stomach. "You're carrying our child, Ella!" His fingers slid over the fabric as if he could somehow caress the child growing beneath her skin. Looking up at her, he asked, "How are you feeling? Is the baby okay? What...?"

Ella cupped his face with her hands, stopping his questions with the gentle caress. "The baby is fine," she told him. "Cassy had her obstetrician come to the palace and he gave me a thorough check up. He listened to the baby's heartbeat, but I wouldn't listen."

"Why not? Do you not want this child?"

She laughed, shaking her head. "I want this child as much as I want you, Malcolm. I just..." she hesitated, blinking back the tears. "I wanted to hear our baby's heartbeat for the first time with you."

He looked up at her, startled and that's when she saw it. He loved her. He truly loved her!

Standing, he took her into his arms once again but this time, his kiss was gentle, slow, and thorough. The only thing that stopped that kiss was a sharp knock on the office door and even then, Malcolm lifted his head, gazing down at Ella with all the love he felt in his heart.

"Thank you," he whispered. "I don't want to miss anything, Ella. I'm excited about this baby," he told her, his large hand covering her stomach. "I want to marry you, but not because of this baby. I promise that I'm going to be a better father than Edward ever was. I'm going to be such a damned good father!" He kissed her again, sealing the words with his actions. "I promise, Ella. Just...don't ever leave me!"

"I won't. I'm sorry that I didn't trust you," she whispered, then shook her head. "No, I'm sorry that I didn't trust us. That I was too scared. You were right. I saw the pain my father went through over the years. It's been so long and he's only just started dating again. I don't want to go through that. I can withstand a lot of crappy stuff," she laughed, then turned serious. "But I don't think I could stand losing you, Malcolm. You're right. I was afraid. But I'm willing to do this as long as you're with me."

"Every step of the way!" he vowed.

Another knock and they both laughed even as they rolled their eyes. "Let's go get this stupid award," she told him. "Then I want you in bed for the next several days."

"Not going to happen," he argued. He opened the door as he said, "Remember? We're getting married tomorrow."

That was the picture that everyone saw in the newspapers the following day; Ella laughing up at her fiancée, a gloriously huge ring on her finger, prominently displayed because her left hand was on his shoulder as they left the hotel manager's office.

Epilogue

Ella walked out of her office and paused, listening for a long moment. Silence? Silence was always bad.

At that moment, Malcolm stepped out of his office as well. He'd been working from home more often as the due date for their fourth child drew near.

"Silence is bad," he said, looking at her from across the hallway.

Ella's hand rubbed over her round belly. "Silence is very bad," she groaned, then waddled around. "Stacy was with the boys this morning," she said, referring to their nanny who took care of their three boys. They were all around two years apart, although this fourth one had been a surprise. Ella and Malcolm had decided that their family was large enough with the three sons and he'd gone through the surgery to take care of the issue. Unfortunately, that exact same day, Ella had discovered that she was pregnant again after fainting when the nurse told her that Malcolm had come out of the surgery and was doing well.

Malcolm moved closer, reaching out to caress her belly. "You, sit down. I'll go find out what's happening."

Ella watched with love in her eyes as Malcolm walked around the corner towards the main part of the house. With three boys, she and Malcolm had designed their current residence so that their individual offices were away from the main part of the house, which had been an excellent idea. Their boys were rowdy, rambunctious, and loud! At ten, eight, and five, her boys were a handful, but she loved every chaotic, crazy moment.

It wasn't until he'd disappeared around the corner that she felt the first pain. It was so strong, she actually doubled over as the contraction rippled over her back and belly. Grabbing onto the wall, she took a deep breath, trying to ride the pain. "Malcolm?" she called out.

Too late. He was gone in search of their brood of loveable hellions.

With careful steps, she walked down the long hallway, relieved when the contraction eased and she could breathe more easily.

Stepping into the great room, she looked around and called out. "Malcolm?"

He appeared on the upper balcony, one boy under each arm and another on his back. All four of them were laughing. Obviously, her boys had ambushed Malcolm, something they loved to do but so far, they'd never managed to pin him down, although the oldest was getting taller and stronger by the day, so their efforts were getting better.

Malcolm took one look at Ella and knew what was going on. "Boys! Starlight!"

With that one word, all three of her boys froze and turned to stare at their mother.

A split second later, she heard all three of them screaming, "Starlight!" Then they were scrambling out of Malcolm's arms, heading towards... she had no idea where.

Malcolm was sprinting down the stairs towards Ella, taking her hands and looking at her carefully. "You think it's time?"

Ella bit her lip, trying to hide her nervousness. "Yes. I think it's time." One would think she'd have this pregnancy and birthing thing down by now. But ever since the moment she'd realized that she was pregnant, this pregnancy had been different.

There was another commotion on the balcony and Ella looked out, seeing her three boys carrying her suitcase down the stairs. One of them could have handled it, but because her boys were overly protective, alpha-male-wannabees, they each carried one corner while Stacy, the nanny, looked on with affectionate concern.

"I've got the boys covered, Ms. Reynolds," Stacy said. "I'll bring them to the hospital once we hear the news."

Ella nodded, relieved to have such a competent woman taking care of her crazy brood. Malcolm was by her side, leading her out of the house. "I've got the keys. The boys have your suitcase. We're set!"

She nodded, feeling another contraction hit her. "I'm scared, Malcolm. This feels different."

"I know, love. We'll get through this together. Stacy said she'd call the hospital for us," he comforted her before he closed the door.

Seven hours later, Ella screamed as their baby daughter made her grand entrance. She already had a tuft of blond hair and was screaming louder than Ella. Malcolm turned to frown at Ella as he said, "A girl?!" Then he passed out on floor of the delivery room.

Ella smiled as one of the nurses placed their baby girl in her arms, another nurse bending down to revive Malcolm, who had been such a trooper during all three of her other pregnancies. Ella just laughed, thinking that this delivery was dramatically different from all of her others, why wouldn't Malcolm react differently as well?

"A girl," she sighed leaning back as she stared down at her little girl. Malcolm was helped up by two of the nurses, who may have been snickering at him. Yeah, Ella was definitely going to tease him about this.

"Do you have a name?" one of the nurses asked.

Ella laughed, shaking her head. "We picked out several names for boys. But nothing for a girl!"

Malcolm had recovered enough so that he could once again stand up. He came over to her and groaned. "Ella, she's a girl!"

Ella laughed. "Nothing gets by you, my big hero!"

Malcolm's large hand came up to curl around their daughter's head. "She's just like her mother," he whispered, awe in his voice.

"Yeah. About time I got some DNA into one of our children," she teased. All three of their sons were smaller versions of Malcolm.

He lifted his eyes, looking right at her. "I love you, Ella."

She smiled, hugging her little daughter close. "I love you too!"

Made in United States
North Haven, CT
25 October 2023